THE MONTAGUE TWINS

THE DEVIL'S MUSIC

NATHAN PAGE & DREW SHANNON

ALFRED A. KNOPF
NEW YORK

To my friends and family, who are always there waiting for me when I return from Narnia

—N.P.

For Sammy, whose love and support is imbued into every single panel

—D.S.

THIS IS A BORZOI BOOK PUBLISHED BY ALFRED A. KNOPF

Jacket design by Ray Shappell

Visit us on the Web! rhcbooks.com

Educators and librarians, for a variety of teaching tools, visit us at RHTeachersLibrarians.com

Library of Congress Cataloging-in-Publication Data is available upon request.
ISBN 978-0-525-64680-8 (trade) — ISBN 978-0-525-64683-9 (ebook) —
ISBN 978-0-525-64681-5 (trade pbk.)

MANUFACTURED IN CHINA
December 2021
10 9 8 7 6 5 4 3 2 1

First Edition

CHAPTER 1

welcome to
PORT HOWL
TICKETS
FALL FAIR '69

PORT HOWL
CENTRAL HIGH

BRRRIING!!
WHAT A STUPID CLASS P.E. IS. JUST A TEACHER SCREAMING AT YOU, "HEY, RUN THERE! NOW RUN HERE! NOW RUN THERE AGAIN!"
AND PEOPLE BLAME THE YOUTH FOR BEING DIRECTIONLESS.
EXACTLY!
RACH, I DON'T KNOW IF WHAT YOU DO COULD BE CONSIDERED RUNNING.
IT'S REALLY MORE OF A CANTER.
A SEDUCTIVE CANTER, THOUGH, RIGHT?
ABSOLUTELY, BABE.

LADIES, CAN YOU BELIEVE WE MADE IT TO FRIDAY?
OH NO, NO, NO . . .
OH YES, YES, YES, WE DID.
NO, I WAS SUPPOSED TO HAND THESE OUT FOR THE SHOW TONIGHT. I'VE BEEN SO BUSY I COMPLETELY FORGOT.
AND HERE THEY COME. GREAT.
GIVE 'EM HERE.
I'LL TAKE CARE OF IT.

OH MY GOD, YOU WILL? THANK YOU!
I'LL COME BY THE STORE TONIGHT AND KEEP YOU COMPANY.
GIRLS, YOU WANT A RIDE HOME?
LET ME GET ONE THING STRAIGHT WITH YOU TWO. IF YOU HUMILIATE MY FRIEND ONSTAGE TONIGHT IN ANY WAY, THE NEXT "CASE" YOU'RE GOING TO BE "SOLVING" IS THE MYSTERY OF WHAT HAPPENED TO YOUR MANHOOD, CAPICHE?
SO YOU BETTER KNOCK 'EM DEAD.
THANKS?
HI, GUYS.
BYE, GUYS.
HI, LAUREL.
BYE, LAUREL.

U SOMEHOW MADE IT WHOLE WEEK WITHOUT URNING IN ANY WORK. ISS ALLEN'S HISTORY PAPER—
EXTENDED A WEEK.
THE MONOLOGUE FOR DRAMA.
THE BANANA BREAD FOR HOME EC?
I'M JUST SAYING, YOU SHOULD TAKE CARE OF THIS STUFF NOW INSTEAD OF WAITING FOR IT TO BITE YOU IN THE ASS.
TOMORROW, AND TOMORROW, AND TOMORROW, I'LL GET IT DONE.
YOU KNOW AS WELL AS I DO YOU HAVE TO WAIT TILL THOSE 'NANNERS ARE BLACK.
CHUCK, PLEASE EXPLAIN TO PETE THAT I'VE GOT EVERYTHING HANDLED.
PETE, HE HAS IT HANDLED.
CHARLIE, PLEASE EXPLAIN TO AL THAT E CAN'T JUST KEEP UTTING THINGS OFF.
AL, STOP PUTTING THINGS OFF.
YOU KNOW WHAT, CHUCK? I NEVER THOUGHT OF IT THAT WAY.
ASS.

THAT'S HER.
SHE'S THE ONE WHO KILLED BRADFORD.
The Hurdy Gurdy Man came singing songs of love,

then when the
HURDY GURDY

SHELLY . . .
SHELLY . . .
SHELLY . . .
SHELLY!

YOU ALL RIGHT, MA? WE WERE CALLING YOU FROM ACROSS THE LOT.
RIGHT AS RAIN, BABE. LET'S LOCOMOTE.

JESUS, GIRL! I COULD HAVE KILLED YOU!
WHO IS THAT?
MILLIE LEFEBVRE. SHE'S A SOPHOMORE.
DOES SHE NEED SOME HELP, YOU THINK? SHE LOOKED . . . OFF.
YOU WOULD TOO IF YOU WERE ESTHER LEFEBVRE'S DAUGHTER.
SHH, MIND YOUR OWN.

Lattimore's SUPERMARKET
OPEN
I'LL SEE YOU THERE TONIGHT?
WITH BELLS ON, LOVE.
HAVE A GOOD SHIFT. SAY HI TO MICK.
and the Wichita lineman is still on the liiiiine
PAY HERE
HI, MR. LATTIMORE. MOM SAYS HI TOO.
CHARLIE, HELLO. NEVER HAS A PERSON BEEN MORE ON TIME.
AND PLEASE, MY BEST TO YOUR MOTHER.
WICHITA LINEMAN - GLENN CA

FLIP!
I'M OFF ON THE DELIVERY RUN. YOU OKAY TO CLOSE UP TONIGHT?
ACTUALLY, WOULD IT BE ALL RIGHT WITH YOU IF I CLOSE UP A LITTLE EARLY? JUST A HALF HOUR OR SO?
WELL, I BEST HAVE A GOOD REASON TO BE TURNING AWAY CUSTOMERS.
MY BAND IS PLAYING TONIGHT AT FAT BLACK CAT.
THOSE MONTAGUE BOYS IN YOUR BAND?
I'M ALMOST AFRAID TO ASK, BUT WHAT DO YOU ALL CALL YOURSELVES?
EXIT
THE BONY FINGERS.

HA HA HA HA HA HA HA
GOOD GOD, I NEEDED THAT.
THAT'S A TERRIBLE NAME.
WELL, TELL YOU WHAT. I'LL MAKE S TO BE BACK BY QUARTER TO SEVE HOW'S THAT?
THAT WOULD BE PERFECT! YOU REALLY DON'T MIND?
NAH. TO SHOOT TRUE WITH YOU, I WAS JUST GOING TO LINGER AROUND THE TAVERN AWHILE AFTER THE LAST DELIVERY. NO REASON I CAN'T WAIT TILL WE CLOSE.
I REALLY APPRECIATE IT.
MAYBE NEXT TIME WE PLAY, YOU CAN COME?
CHARLIE, I WON'T GILD THE LILY, I'M NO FAN OF ROCK-AND-ROLL MUSIC.
BUT YOU KNOCK 'EM DEAD.

REMEMBER TO SPEAK ONLY TRUTH. THE SHADOWS WILL CALL OUT A LIE.
ROWAN, I . . .
I DIDN'T SEE THIS GETTING QUITE SO OUT OF HAND, IT'S JUST . . .
I'M SORRY.
IT'S, UM . . .
IT MIGHT STILL BE FINE?
I MEAN, WE ARE WHERE WE ARE, RIGHT?
AND IF WE HADN'T BEEN THERE? WHO KNOWS?
YOU'RE RIGHT. OF COURSE. LET'S WAIT UNTIL WE HAVE ALL OF THE INFORMATION BEFORE . . .

ISN'T THAT IT, THOUGH?
WE'LL NEVER HAVE ALL OF THE INFORMATION.
WE ANSWER TO THESE SHADOWS WE CALL THE FACULTY.
THEY ANSWER TO THEIR SHADOWS.
AND THOSE SHADOWS ANSWER TO THEIR SHADOWS.
ROUND AND ROUND THE MYSTERY GOES, WHERE IT STOPS, NOBODY KNOWS.
AND SO WE STUDY MAGIC SO THAT WE CAN, WHAT?
SPICE UP THE MUNDANE?
YOU KNOW AS WELL AS I DO, ROWAN, THAT IT'S MORE THAN THAT.
A DOCTOR WHO HAS STUDIED MAGIC WILL BE BETTER ABLE TO HEAL.
MAGIC IS A DEEPER LEVEL OF HUMAN UN-DERSTANDING.
THEN WHY ARE THERE SO FEW OF US?

WHY IS IT THAT A PERSON WHO HAS WITNESSED A SUPERNATURAL EVENT WILL JUST FORGET IT?
NOT REMEMBERING SOMETHING IS NOT THE SAME AS FORGETTING IT.
OH, COME ON, DAVE!
IF IT'S A EPER LEVEL OF HUMAN NDERSTANDING, THEN Y ARE WE, AS HUMANS, EMINGLY NOT MEANT TO UNDERSTAND IT?
I'M TRYING TO TEACH YOUR KIDS, MAN. THEY TRUST ME.
THEY THINK I WITHHOLD ANSWERS BECAUSE THEY AREN'T READY.
THE TRUTH IS, MOST OF THE TIME, I HAVEN'T GOT A GODDAMN CLUE WHAT TO TELL THEM.
I CAN RELATE.
MY HOPE IS, AFTER TONIGHT, WE'LL BE ABLE TO BE MORE HONEST WITH THEM.
DO YOU REGRET TAKING IT UP? THE APPRENTICESHIP? THE TEACHING?
I DON'T REGRET IT.
I JUST WISH IT DIDN'T FEEL SO MUCH LIKE SHADOWBOXING.
I AM HAPPY YOU HAVE QUESTIONS. AND I WANT US TO PICK THIS BACK UP.
BUT RIGHT NOW, WE HAVE TO GO BOX SHADOWS.

SCIENTIA POTENTIA EST.
CA-CHUNK
TK
TK
TK
TK

YOU'RE UP.
INCIPIT VITA NOVA!

NICE JOB.
NO PAPER CUTS
THIS TIME.
NEVER
AGAIN.

REMEMBER, SPEAKING TO ONE ANOTHER IN WHISPERS IS NOT AN OPTION.
THE WAY THE ROOM IS CONSTRUCTED, SOUND CARRIES IN A TERRIFYING WAY.
IF THE PERSON TALKING HAS LIED, THE SOUND THE SHADOWS RETURN WILL BE DEAFENING. IF THE PERSON HAS TOLD THE TRUTH, THERE IS HARDLY AN ECHO.
DAVID, I KNOW ALL OF THIS.
Faculty Office
EVEN SO.

APPROACH.

CAT RECORD
Creem
HEY, TENNYSON, WHERE SHOUL WE PUT OUR STUFF?
PROBABLY IN YOUR GARAGE?
NO, WE'RE PLAYING TONIGHT. . . .
I HAVE NO EARTHLY IDEA WH YOU'RE TALKING ABOUT, MAN.
HEY, GUYS. I'M THINKING THERE MAY BE SOME CONFUSION.

YEAH, LIKE TENNYSON SAYING HE HAS NO IDEA THERE'S A SHOW IN HIS SHOP TONIGHT.
TECHNICALLY, HE DOESN'T. *YET.*
HE *WHAT?!*
TENNYSON, WHEN WE FOUND THAT RARE PRESSING OF "MY HAPPINESS" THAT WAS STOLEN, YOU SAID YOU'D PAY US IN STORE CREDIT, CORRECT?
YEAH, I MEANT, LIKE, RECORDS, MAGAZINES. . . .
TATION
THIS IS HOW I WOULD LIKE TO USE MY STORE CREDIT. IT'S THE FIRST NIGHT OF THE FALL FAIR, SO YOU KNOW THERE WILL BE TRAFFIC. WE'VE GOT THREE ACTS LINED UP, INCLUDING OURSELVES. WHEN ALL IS SAID AND DONE, YOU'LL ONLY BE OPEN AN HOUR LATER THAN USUAL.
I SUGGEST YOU KEEP THAT REGISTER READY, BECAUSE WE'RE ABOUT TO INSPIRE A GENERATION OF CONSUMERS.

SIIIIGH
I GET HUNDRED PERCENT DOOR.
TEN PERCENT.
EIGHTY.
I GOTTA GIVE THE BANDS SOMETHING, MAN.
SEVENTY-FIVE OF THE DOOR, FINAL OFFER.
THAT'S A DEAL.
COME ON, PETE, LET'S GET THE REST OF THE GEAR.
CLOSED
HOW MUCH ARE WE CHARGING ANYWAY?
NOTHING. FREE GIG.

DO YOU KNOW WHY YOU HAVE BEEN CALLED?

SPEAKER, I LONG AGO LEARNED TO STOP TRYING TO FORETELL THE MOTIVES OF THE FACULTY.

YOU HAVE BEEN BROUGHT BEFORE THE FACULTY FOR YOUR INVOLVEMENT IN THE DEATH OF ONE OF ITS MEMBERS, AMONG OTHER SUSPICIONS TO BE ADDRESSED SHORTLY.
BUT TO BEGIN . . .

TELL ME, BOTH OF YOU: YOUR WIFE, YOUR FRIEND, DID SHE KNOWINGLY TARGET A MEMBER OF THE FACULTY?
NO WAY.
ABSOLUTELY NOT.
SO IT IS A COINCIDENCE, DAVID, THAT YOUR WIFE WAS THE DRIVER IN THE COLLISION THAT KILLED ROGER BRADFORD?
IT WAS AN ACCIDENT.
ACCIDENT
ACCIDENT
ACCIDENT
ACCIDENT

NO, THAT'S NOT . . .
SHE HAD TO DO IT. IT WAS SELF-DEFENSE. A FULL INVESTIGATION BY THE AUTHORITIES CORROBORATED THAT.
ROGER BRADFORD THREATENED THE LIVES OF MY CHILDREN AND WOULD HAVE KILLED MY WIFE. ASIDE FROM THAT, HAD WE NOT BEEN THERE, HE WOULD HAVE MURDERED HIS OWN DAUGHTER.
COULD THE QUESTION NOT BE ASKED: WAS THE FACULTY TARGETING *MY FAMILY*?
WE ARE QUITE AWARE OF THE SEQUENCE OF EVENTS. YES. QUITE.
WE NEED TO SPEAK TO THE CHILDREN.

BUT WHY SHOULD YOU NEED—
TELL ME, ARE THEY NOT AWARE OF THE PRACTICE OF MAGIC?
THEY ARE.
HAVE THEY NOT ALL *USED* MAGIC THEMSELVES?
IN FACT, WAS IT NOT THE MISUSE OF THE CRAFT THAT BEGAN THE TRAGIC CIRCUMSTANCES WE NOW DISCUSS?
YES. THEY HAVE. IT WAS.

GRUMBLE
MURMUR
MURMUR
MURMUR GRUMBLE
MURMUR
YET WE UNDERSTAND THAT THE ENTIRE THESIS OF MR. ROWAN DAVIS HINGES ON THE VERY IDEA THAT WE SHOULD BE TEACHING YOUNGER?
BRING US THE CHILDREN.
LET US SEE WHAT YOUR LITTLE LESSONS HAVE PRODUCED.
BUT I'M NOT READY. THEY AREN'T READ—
THIS MEETING IS ADJOURNED.
THE FACULTY HAS OTHER MATTERS TO ADDRESS THIS EVENING.
WE WILL BE IN TOUCH.

THIS IS WHAT THEY PAY YOU FOR AROUND HERE?
HEY, RACH.
CAME TO SEE HOW YOU'RE DOING BEFORE THE BIG SHOW.
WANNA COME OUT FOR A SMOKE?
YOU KNOW I DON'T SMOKE.
YES, YES, I KNOW. WHAT I MEANT WAS, DO YOU WANT TO COME WATCH ME SMOKE?

UNLESS YOU NEED TO TAKE CARE OF THIS LINE FIRST?
I LOVE THIS TIME OF YEAR.
THIS WEEK 15¢/lb
RK CHOPS
OPEN
WE ALWAYS GET THIS FIVE-DAY STRETCH IN THE FALL WHERE IT'S JUST PERFECT.
DREARY BUT WITH A BIT OF SUN THROUGH THE DAY. CHILLY BUT WARM ENOUGH TO JUST WEAR A LIGHT JACKET AT NIGHT.
THOSE FIVE DAYS ARE MY FAVORITE SEASON.
HOW ARE YOU DOING, RACH?
PEACHY KEEN, JELLY BEAN.
THAT ACTUALLY DOESN'T SOUND VERY REASSURING COMING FROM YOU.

HONESTLY. I FEEL . . . GOOD.
YEAH, YOU DO?
I MEAN, THAT'S GREAT.
HOW HAS IT BEEN WITH YOUR STEPMOM?
THE WICKED STEPMOM ISN'T SO WICKED. MY DAD WAS TERRIBLE TO HER TOO. HE WAS . . . VERY GOOD AT KEEPING US APART.
SHE DIDN'T SIGN UP TO RAISE A SEVENTEEN-YEAR-OLD DAUGHTER, THOUGH. SHE'S HARDLY EVER THERE.
HERE'S THE WEIRD THING. I THINK SHE'S PART OF THE REASON I'VE BEEN DOING SO WELL.
OH?
DON'T TELL THE GIRLS AND TWINS, OKAY?
SHE SET ME UP WITH HER THERAPIST.
I THINK THAT'S AMAZING, RACH.

HOW'S JESPER?
WE, UM, HAD TO LET HIM GO FOR A LITTLE WHILE.
WHAT? WHY?
THE ESTATE IS A LITTLE COMPLICATED RIGHT NOW. LAWYERS ARE HANDLING IT ALL. I'LL BRING HIM BACK AS SOON AS IT GETS SORTED.
I THINK YOU'VE GOT A CUSTOMER.

YOU WORRIED WE'RE GONNA STEAL YOUR CAR OR SOMETHING, MISTER?

FORCE OF HABIT. FORGOT I'M NOT IN THE CITY ANYMORE.
OH, WE WERE ABSOLUTELY GOING TO STEAL YOUR CAR.
WELL, AREN'T YOU TROUBLE?
NO, I'M RACHEL. AND THIS IS CHARLIE.
A PLEASURE, RACHEL, CHARLIE.
I'M GIDEON.
DON'T MIND HER. WHAT RACHEL LACKS IN SOCIAL GRACE SHE MAKES UP FOR IN, I DON'T KNOW, SOMETHING, I'M SURE.
WHAT BRINGS YOU TO PORT HOWL, GIDEON?

BIG PICTURE OR LITTLE PICTURE?
BOTH.
BIG PICTURE? SCENERY CHANGE. BOSTON WAS FEELING KIND OF GRAY.
LITTLE PICTURE?
I'M HERE FOR GROCERIES.
OPEN
ICE
WELL, CONSIDER US YOUR WELCOMING COMMITTEE.
JUST MY LUCK. FIRST PEOPLE I ME ARE A COUPLE OF DEVIOUS CAR THIEVES.
WHEREABOUTS ARE YOU STAYING?
WHY, WANT TO ROB ME TOO?
I'M RENTING A PLACE FROM A MRS. NORMANDY.
SAY, GIDEON, YOU STRIKE ME AS SOMEONE WHO ENJOYS GOOD MUSIC.
YOU FLATTER ME.
HOW WOULD YOU LIKE TO SEE THE HOTTEST UP-AND-COMING BAND IN ALL NEW ENGLAND?
IN CONCERT
The BONY FINGERS
FAT BLACK CAT
FRI. OCT. 10 | 8PM

PORT HOWL FALL FAIR '69
TICKETS
OUR CHILDREN ARE BEING BRAINWASHED!
MOTHERS AGAINST ROCK & ROLL
FAT BLACK CAT
Fletcher's

WHERE'VE YOU BEEN?
WE WERE SUMMONED BY THE FACULTY.
THEY KNOW EVERYTHING.

ABOUT YOU, ABOUT BRADFORD.
AND THE KIDS.
THEY WANT TO SEE THE KIDS, SHELLY.
HON, DID YOU HEAR ME?
I MUST NOT HAVE.
BECAUSE WHAT IT SOUNDS LIKE IS THAT SOME ASSHOLES IN THEIR HOUSECOATS ARE TALKING ABOUT WHAT HAPPENED TO *ME*—DEMANDING TO SEE *MY* CHILDREN—WITHOUT THE BASE LEVEL OF DECENCY TO SAY ANY OF IT TO MY FACE.
DID I HEAR YOU RIGHT, *HON?*
SOUNDS LIKE, YEP.
WELL, PUT ON YOUR DANCING SHOES, BOYS.
FIRST, WE'RE GOING TO CUT A RUG HERE.
THEN WE'RE TAKING A SPIN OVER TO THE FACULTY.

ALL RIGHT, GANG. THIS IS IT. WHAT ARE WE GONNA DO?
WE DON'T HAVE TIME FOR THIS, WE NEED TO GET OUT THERE.
LET'S JUST GET IT OUT OF THE WAY. . . .
I'M NOT.
WELL, I'M NOT STARTING UNTIL YOU SAY IT.
CHARLIE?
NO, SCREW THAT.
AL, CHARLIE AND I ARE READY TO—
YOU TOO, CHUCK.
WE ARE READY TO MAKE SOME MAGIC.

LET'S MAKE SOME MAGIC.
WOOOO!!!
CLAP
CLAP
CLAP
CLAP
CLAP
GO GROOVY FINGERS!
BONY FINGERS.
GO BONY FINGERS!
CLAP
YA!
CLAP
CLAP
WOOHOO!
CLAP

HI, WE'RE THE BONY FINGERS, AS YOU JUST HEARD MY DAD YELL.
WE'VE GOT A COUPLE OF ORIGINALS AND SOME COVERS.
STARTING WITH THIS ONE. SING ALONG IF YOU KNOW IT.
SUGAR . . .
BUM BUM BUM BUM
BUM BUM
OHHHH, HONEY, HONEY . . .

CHAPTER 2

THANK YOU, GOOD NIGHT!
CLAP
CLAP
CLAP
YA!
CLAP
CLAP
WOOHOO
CLAP
CLAP
CLAP
CLAP
CLAP
CLAP
CLAP
CLAP
CLAP
CLAP
CLAP
OU GUYS WERE SO GOOD!
THAT WAS SO MUCH BETTER THAN I WAS EXPECTING.
CONGRATULATIONS, MONTAGUES. YOU DIDN'T SUCK.
WERE WE OKAY?
BETTER THAN OKAY. I THINK I ACTUALLY HAD FUN TONIGHT.
KEEP IT DOWN, RACH, YOU'VE GOT AN IMAGE TO PRESERVE.

LISTEN, A BUNCH OF US ARE GOING TO WALK AROUND THE FAIR.
THEN MAYBE TO THE BEACH FOR A BONFIRE.
YOU ALL SHOULD COME.
SURE!
HEY, WHO'S THAT?
WHO?
HUH. I CAN'T QUITE PUT MY FINGER ON IT. SUPER FAMILIAR, THOUGH.
CHUCK, DO YOU KNOW THAT GUY?
OH MY GOD, HE ACTUALLY CAME.

THAT'S SOME GUY WHO JUST GOT INTO TOWN. RACHEL WAS GIVING HIM THE HARD SELL ON THE SHOW WHEN HE CAME IN TO GET GROCERIES.
HIS NAME'S GORDON OR SOMETHING. KNOW IT STARTED WITH A G.
WAIT A MINUTE.
G-H
Gray Harbor
GIDEON. HIS NAME IS GIDEON DRAKE.
HE WAS IN ONE OF THE BIGGEST UP-AND-COMING BANDS.
WAS?
HE LEFT THE BAND.
LOTS OF RUMORS ABOUT WHY, BUT BOILS DOWN TO THE SAME OLD STORY.
HE WANTED TO GO SOLO.
RACH, DID YOU KNOW THIS GUY WAS A ROCK STAR?
ARE YOU KIDDING? OF COURSE I KNEW.

OHMYGODOHMYGOD, HE'S COMING OVER HERE, WHAT DO WE DO?
AL, LOOK AT YOU, YOU'RE RATTLED.
JUST BE COOL. ACT NATURAL.
GIDEON DRAKE, I'M A PLEASURE TO MEET YOU.
I MEAN . . .
COME ON, BIG GUY.
MR. DRAKE, THIS IS MY BROTHER, AL. HE'S A BIG FAN.
GIDEON, PLEASE. AND LIKEWISE. I QUITE ENJOYED YOUR SET.
WHAT DID I TELL YOU? WEREN'T THEY GOOD?
YOU WERE RIGHT. YOU'RE AN HONEST CAR THIEF. THANK YOU FOR THE INVITATION.

WELL, I SHOULD BE GOING. IT WAS NICE TO MEET ALL OF YOU.
WE'RE GOING TO WALK AROUND THE FAIR. THEN MAYBE TO THE BEACH FOR A BONFIRE.
YOU SHOULD COME.

MAYBE GET A LITTLE MUSIC?
Y'ALL CAN JUST SIT IN IT.

DO YOU REALLY THINK THIS IS A GOOD IDEA?
STORMING IN THERE AND TEARING A STRIP OFF THE FACULTY?
I'M NOT GOING IN THERE TO TEAR A STRIP OFF ANYBODY.
I'M GOING IN THERE TO CONFESS.
YOU'RE WHAT?
IF THEY WANT TO BLAME SOMEONE FOR ROGER'S DEATH, IT'S GOING TO BE ME.
I DID IT.
AND I WOULD DO IT AGAIN. I'D DO IT A HUNDRED TIMES OUT OF A HUNDRED.
SO LET'S JUST GET THIS OUT OF THE WAY.

YOU SURE IT'S OKAY? I CAN TRY TO WIN YOU A BIGGER ONE.
IT'S PERFECT. AND YOU'RE THE ONLY PRIZE I REALLY WANTED ANYWAY.
DO YOU LIKE YOURS?
NO, I TOLD YOU THAT STUPID GAME WAS RIGGED. NOW COME HERE.
WHO'S ALIGNED TO IGNORE THAT SIDE OF THE FIRE FOR THE REST OF THE NIGHT?
AYE.
YEP.
ALIGNED.
SPEAK FOR YOURSELF, SHIT *JUST* GOT INTERESTING.

YOU WITH US?

YEAH.

YOU EVER SEE A *STAR IS BORN*?
NO. ANY GOOD?
IT'S MY FAVORITE MOVIE. THIS HOLLYWOOD POWER COUPLE WHOSE STARS ARE HEADING IN OPPOSITE DIRECTIONS.
HE'S PAST HIS PRIME, TOTAL LUSH. LIKE, CRASHING-THE-OSCARS TYPE OF DRU TREATS HER LIKE COMPL SHIT BECAUSE SHE'S YO AND HOT AND EVERYO WANTS HER. AND AL SHE WANTS IS HIM.
WHY?
HE WONDERS THAT HIMSELF.

SO WHAT HAPPENS? DO THEY END UP HAPPILY EVER AFTER?
THEY GO THEIR SEPARATE WAYS.
YOU CAN TALK TO HIM, YOU KNOW. HE'S JUST A GUY WHO MADE SOME MUSIC.
SOME MUSIC?
IT'S NOT JUST SOME MUSIC, IT'S . . .
YOU KNOW WHEN YOU TAKE A STEEP HILL IN A CAR GOING JUST A LITTLE TOO FAST? THAT FEELING IN YOUR STOMACH? I GET THAT WHEN I LISTEN TO HIS SONGS. THEY SET SOMETHING RIGHT IN ME.
BUT WHEN I LOOK AT HIM NOW? I CAN'T SHAKE THE FEELING THERE'S SOMETHING OFF.
LIKE HE SHOULDN'T BE HERE.
I SHOULD REALLY LISTEN TO IT.

WOULD YOU WANT TO COME OVER AND LISTEN TO IT SOMETIME?
I THINK I SEE SOMEONE AT THE LIGHTHOUSE.
LOOK, IS THAT SOMEONE STANDING ON THE ROCKS OVER THERE?
NOW, WHO THE HELL WOULD BE CRAZY ENOUGH . . .
LET'S GO FIND OUT.
HEY, IS EVERYTHING ALL RIGHT?
I SAID ARE YOU OKAY?
I THINK THAT'S MILL FROM SCHOOL. SAW HER EARL AND SHE SEEM REALLY OUT OF IT.

SHIT, YOU'RE RIGHT.
MILLIE, COME ON DOWN FROM THERE!

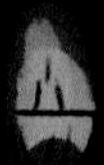

I WOULD UNDERSTAND IF YOU WANTED TO WAIT OUT HERE.
I WOULD FOLLOW YOU INTO HELL ITSELF. YOU KNOW THAT.
COME ON. WHATEVER HAPPENS ON THE OTHER SIDE OF THAT DOOR, WE FACE IT TOGETHER.

YOU SWEAR TO DO ALL IN YOUR POWER TO MAINTAIN BALANCE AND ORDER.
I DO.
YOU WILL BE UNCOMPROMISING ON THAT WHICH SERVES TO CREATE DISCORD BETWEEN THE MAGIC AND THE MUNDANE.
I WILL.
RISE, THEN, AND TAKE YOUR SEAT AT THE INQUISITORS' TABLE.
ELI MONTAGUE, WELCOME TO OUR CHAPTER.
WELCOME TO THE FACULTY.
SHELLY, DAVID . . .
WHAT IMPECCABLE TIMING.

WHAT'S SHE SAYING?
SHE'S SHIVERING TOO MUCH, I CAN'T MAKE IT OUT.
JESUS, MILLIE! WHAT HAPPENED? WHAT WERE YOU DOING?
I THOUGHT I SAW SOMEONE OUT THERE.
IS SHE OKAY?
I THINK EVERYONE'S ALL RIGHT. BUT, GUYS, THIS GIRL IS, LIKE, CATATONIC. SHE HASN'T BLINKED.

WHAT'S SHE SAYING?
WE CAN'T MAKE IT OUT.
WHAT HAPPENED?
LA-LA . . . LA LA-LA . . . LA LA-LA LA LA . . . I . . . ALONE . . .

HEY, WHAT'S THAT YOU'RE SINGING, MILLIE?
SHE'S FREEZING, WE NEED TO GET HER INSIDE.
I KNOW SOMEONE WE CAN CALL.
WHO IS SHE? DO YOU KNOW HER?
FROM SCHOOL. SHE'S A GRADE BELOW US.

RACH, DON'S GOING TO TAKE US HOME. I WAS SUPPOSED TO BE BACK ALMOST AN HOUR AGO.
HAVE A GOOD NIGHT, GIRLS. CALL YOU TOMORROW.
HEY, WHERE'S GIDEON?
HE WAS RIGHT HERE A SECOND AGO.
YOU DID THE RIGHT THING CALLING ME. SHE'S IN A BAD WAY.
WHAT DO YOU THINK HAPPENED TO HER?

ELL, HATE TO SAY IT, BUT IT COULD BE RUGS. SEEN IT BEFORE. TAKE A BAD HIT, EOPLE CAN SNAP. SOMETIMES THEY COME ACK, SOMETIMES THEY JUST TAY LIKE THAT.

THEN THERE'S THE MUTTERING. NEAR AS I CAN MAKE OUT, SHE KEEPS SAYING SOMETHING ABOUT BEING ALL ALONE.

I'VE ALREADY GOT A CAR ON THE WAY TO HER PARENTS. WE'LL GET THEM TO MEET US AT THE HOSPITAL.

Y'ALL SHOULD GO HOME. GET SOME SLEEP.

UM, AL. A WORD OF ADVICE? HAVE A CUP OF COFFEE OR SOMETHING IN YA BEFORE YOU GO HOME. IN CASE DAVID AND SHELLY ARE AWAKE.

I WON'T MENTION THE BOOZE UNLESS THEY ASK ME.

THINK YOU AND YOUR POSSE MIGHT HAVE SAVED A GIRL TONIGHT.

APPRECIATE THAT, OFFICER.

TEN-THIRTY ON A FRIDAY NIGHT, THOUGH? THEY'RE DEFINITELY ASLEEP.

MY FEET AREN'T FEETING RIGHT.
DAMN FEET.
I KNOW, BUDDY, DAMN THOSE CURSED FEET OF YOURS.
YOU GUYS EVER SEE THIS CAR BEFORE?
NEVER. BUT IT MEANS MOM AND DAD ARE STILL UP, SO ANY HOPE OF GETTING THIS ONE INSIDE WITHOUT THEM NOTICING IS SHOT.
AL, WE NEED YOU TO PATCH TOGETHER TWO MINUTES OF RELATIVE SOBRIETY. DO YOU THINK YOU CAN DO THAT?

SLAP ME.
I'M NOT GOING TO SLAP YOU.
IT'S THE ONLY WAY.
C'MON, REALLY PUT SOME MUSTARD ON IT.
I'M NOT SLAPPING—
SLAP ME!
STOP ASKING ME TO—
SMACK!!
CHUCK, YOU ARE A TRUE FRIEND.

TRIP!

KIDS, CAN WE SEE YOU IN THE KITCHEN?
IS THAT SLAP STILL ON THE TABLE?
IT'S NOT MY FAULT!
WHO PUT THESE PONTOONS RIGHT BY THE STAIRS?

HI THERE. I'M PETER MONTAGUE.
IT IS A PLEASURE TO FINALLY MEET YOU, PETER.

AND THAT MUST MAKE YOU ALASTAIR.
MY NAME IS ELI.
S'PLEASURE.
BOYS, THIS IS ELI MONTAGUE.
HE IS YOUR UNCLE.
WE DON'T HAVE AN UNCLE.

NO, YOU WERE NEVER TOLD YOU HAVE AN UNCLE.
DON'T.
DON'T YOU DARE.
DAVID? DID YOU KNOW?
YES.
SOMEBODY NEEDS TO EXPLAIN JUST WHAT THE FUCK IS GOING ON.
ALASTAIR!
PERHAPS WE SHOULD TAKE THIS TO THE LIVING ROOM? NOT SUCH CLOSE QUARTERS.

NO, I THINK WE CAN DISCUSS IT RIGHT HERE.
THIS IS ELI. HE IS, BY BLOOD, YOUR UNCLE. BUT ONLY BY BLOOD.
VERY WELL, AL.
HE AND FRANCIS HAD NOT SPOKEN FOR YEARS BEFORE YOU TWO WERE BORN.
I DIDN'T HAVE A CHOICE. IT WAS FRANCIS AND OUR FATHER WHO HAD THE FALLING-OUT. I WAS CAUGHT IN THE MIDDLE, EXPECTED TO MAKE A CHOICE BETWEEN THEM.
HI! HELLO. ONCE AGAIN, BIG PLEASURE TO MEET YOU AFTER SEVENTEEN YEARS!
WHAT AL IS SAYING IS THAT IT LOOKS LIKE YOU MADE YOUR CHOICE.

HAVE YOU TOLD THEM ANYTHING ABOUT US? ABOUT THE MONTAGUES?
IF THEIR OWN FATHER FOUND NO REASON TO DO SO, WHAT RIGHT WAS IT OF MINE?
WELL, THAT'S AWFULLY CONVENIENT FOR YOU, ISN'T IT?
WHAM!
WHAT ABOUT ANY OF THIS DO YOU THINK HAS BEEN CONVENIENT FOR ME? FOR THEM? FOR MY FAMILY?
WHAT I FIND CONVENIENT, ELI, IS THAT YOU WALTZ IN HER TONIGHT OUT OF, WHAT A SUDDEN CONCERN FO YOUR NEPHEWS?
WE'VE BEEN HERE. THE WHOLE DAMN TIME.
AND A FINE JOB YOU'VE DONE TOO. REBEL WITHOUT A CAUSE OVER THERE IS CLEARLY BLOTTO.
ARE WE REALLY GOING TO FOCUS ON THIS RIGHT NOW? AREN'T THERE MORE PRESSING MATTERS AT HAND?
YOU PLAY ONE CONCERT AND YOU THINK YOU'RE KEITH RICHARDS? NUH-UH. WE'RE TALKING ABOUT THIS LATER, MISTER.

LOOK, I'VE CLEARLY CAUSED A BIT OF A STIR BY COMING HERE.
THAT WASN'T MY INTENTION.
OBVIOUSLY YOU ALL HAVE A LOT TO TALK ABOUT. I'M GOING TO GET OUT OF YOUR HAIR.
IT LOOKS LIKE I'M GOING TO BE AROUND PORT HOWL FOR THE FORESEEABLE FUTURE.
IF EITHER OF YOU EVER WANTS TO COME TALK TO ME, THIS IS WHERE I'LL BE.
OH, AND, DAVID . . .
I'LL SEE YOU AROUND THE OFFICE.
I CAN LET MYSELF OUT.

ALASTAIR MONTAGUE, YOU HAVE THE AUDACITY TO COME INTO THIS HOUSE DRUNK?
PETER, CHARLIE, WHAT DO YOU TWO HAVE TO SAY FOR YOURSELVES? SUPPOSE YOU'RE DRUNK AS WELL.
I'M NOT DRUNK. IF I'M ACTING AWKWARD, IT'S ONLY BECAUSE THIS SITUATION IS VERY UNCOMFORTABLE.
WE HAVE AN UNCLE THAT YOU COMPLETELY NEGLECTED TO TELL US ABOUT, AND WHAT YOU WANT TO FOCUS ON IS THAT I HAD SOMETHING TO DRINK? IS THAT SERIOUSLY WHERE WE'RE AT?
WHAT DID ELI MEAN WHEN HE ASKED IF YOU HAD TOLD US ABOU THE MONTAGUES? WHAT HAVEN'T YOU TOLD US?

AY, HERE'S HOW WE'RE GOING TO DO THIS. WE CAN ONLY
E ONE OF THESE CONVERSATIONS, AND CERTAINLY, AL, YOU
E CORRECT IN THAT WE SHOULD BE WASTING NO TIME ON
THE ISSUE OF YOUR INEBRIATION.
THANK YOU, THAT'S WHAT I'M SAYING.
YOU'RE GROUNDED A WEEK. YOU CAN GO TO SCHOOL, YOU CAN GO TO ROWAN'S LESSONS. OTHER THAN THAT? NADA.
COMPRENDE?
WHAM

DAVID, I AM SO . . .
EVERYONE IN THE LIVING ROOM, PLEASE. EXCEPT YOU, AL.
LOOK AT ME.
YOU'RE GOING TO FIX THAT. IN FACT, I THINK THE WHOLE KITCHEN COULD USE A FRESH COAT OF PAINT. WHAT DO YOU THINK?
YES, DAVID. AM I GROUNDED LONGER?

O, AL, YOU'RE NOT. BUT I EED YOU TO UNDERSTAND SOMETHING.
IF YOU EVER THROW ANOTHER FIST IN THIS HOUSE, YOU WON'T NEED TO WORRY ABOUT BEING GROUNDED, YOU'LL BE OUT ON YOUR ASS.
I WON'T HAVE ANYONE IN HIS FAMILY FEELING UNSAFE IN THEIR OWN HOME.
YOU'RE TOO OLD TO BE THROWING TANTRUMS.
YOU SHOULD GET SOME ICE ON THAT.
I'M GOING INTO THE LIVING ROOM TO HAVE A DIFFICULT BUT RATIONAL CONVERSATION.
IF YOU THINK YOU'RE PREPARED TO JOIN US, PLEASE DO.
IF WE'RE GOING TO GET MORE OF THAT BEHAVIOR, YOU CAN JUST GO TO YOUR ROOM.

I COUNT MYSELF AMONG THE FEW YOUR FATHER WOULD SPEAK TO ABOUT HIS FAMILY.

UNDERSTAND THAT IF FRANCIS HAD HAD ONE, JUST *ONE*, REDEEMING THING TO SAY ABOUT THEM, I WOULD HAVE HESITATED TO KEEP WHAT I HAVE FROM YOU.

WHY DID THEY FALL OUT? OUR DAD AND HIS FAMILY.
BEFORE YOUR PARENTS, THE MONTAGUE NAME HAD A MUCH DIFFERENT MEANING TO PRACTITIONERS.
IT WAS A NAME TO BE FEARED.
THE MONTAGUES, ALONG WITH THE BRADFORDS, WERE SOME OF THE FIRST INQUISITORS OF THE AMERICAS.
INQUISITORS?
WITCH HUNTERS.
THE BLOODSHED BETWEEN THE PRACTITIONERS AND THE INQUISITORS RAGED ON FOR HUNDREDS OF YEARS.
IT DID NOT BEGIN, NOR DID IT END, WITH THE TRIALS.
IT WAS ONLY ON THE EVE OF OUR COUNTRY ENTERING THE SECOND WORLD WAR THAT AN ACCORD WAS FINALLY REACHED.
THOUGH THE TERM WASN'T COINED UNTIL QUITE RECENTLY, BOTH SIDES UNDERSTOOD THAT TO KEEP FIGHTING WOULD MEAN MUTUAL ASSURED DESTRUCTION. THIS IS HOW THE FACULTY WAS BORN.

HAS ROWAN TOLD YOU MUCH ABOUT THE FACULTY?
NOT MUCH, BUT THEY'VE COME UP. HE USUALLY CUTS HIMSELF OFF THE MOMENT HE REALIZES HE'S TALKING ABOUT THEM.
BLAH, BLAH, BLAH, MYSTERIOUS COMMENT, FOLLOWED BY THE WHOLE MUSTN'T-DISCUSS-IT THING.
THE FACULTY OF PORT HOWL IS COMPOSED OF SEVEN MEMBERS THREE PRACTITIONERS. THREE INQUISITORS. AND A SPEAKER, THE FINAL WORD IN ALL MATTERS.
THERE ARE CHAPTERS THROUGHOUT NORTH AMERICA. AROUND THE WORL THERE ARE MANY DIFFERING SYSTEM ALL ULTIMATELY WITH THE SAME PURPOSE.
WAIT A MINUTE. WHY ARE WE HEARING THIS FROM YOU? I THOUGHT YOU WEREN'T ABLE TO TALK TO US ABOUT THIS STUFF. UNLESS . . .
THEY ALREADY KNOW.

DON'T UNDERSTAND. WHAT DOES
AT MEAN? FOR US? FOR ROWAN?
WHAT DOES THAT MEAN FOR YOU, DAD?
HONESTLY? WE DON'T KNOW YET.
THEY WANT TO MEET YOU.
ALL OF YOU.
SORRY, NOT TO PUT OUT ONE FIRE WITH ANOTHER, BUT WHAT DOES ANY OF THIS HAVE TO DO WITH OUR FAMILY? WITH THE MONTAGUES?
EVERYTHING.

YOUR GRANDFATHER ARTEMIS WAS STEADFASTLY MIRED IN THE OLD WAYS.
"ALL HERETICS BURN, IN THIS LIFE OR THE NEXT," HE WAS FOND OF SAYING.
SO YOU KNEW HIM
NO, THANK GOODNESS. HE SAID SO REPEATEDLY IN HIS WRITINGS.
WRITINGS?
FOR HIM, ALLOWING ANY MAGIC TO EXIST WAS BLASPHEMOUS, PLAIN AND SIMPLE. YET FOR ALL HIS VITRIOL TOWARD IT, THE MAN WAS OBSESSED WITH THE SUPERNATURAL.
WHERE DID I LEAVE THAT . . .
AH YES, HERE IT IS.
A.S. MONTAGUE

E WROTE BOOKS ON WITCHES, HOSTS, DEMONS, YOU NAME IT. ING SPECIAL ATTENTION ON HOW BEST TO ERADICATE THEM.

WHEREAS MOST OF HIS CONTEMPORARIES WOULD SIMPLY PUBLISH WITHIN COMMUNITIES THAT WERE AWARE OF THE EXISTENCE OF SUCH THINGS, ARTEMIS RELEASED HIS BOOKS TO THE PUBLIC AT LARGE, PAYING FOR THE PRODUCTION OUT OF HIS OWN POCKET.

THEY WERE DIVISIVE BOOKS, WITH MANY PEOPLE ASSUMING THEY WERE SIMPLY THE RANTINGS OF A MADMAN.

MANY OTHERS, HOWEVER, REVERED THEM AS HIGH CTION. SOMETHING AKIN TO AM STOKER'S JOURNALISTIC STYLE IN *DRACULA*.

MOST CREATURE FEATURES YOU SEE NOW ARE INDEBTED IN SOME WAY TO THE BOOKS YOUR GRANDFATHER WROTE, THOUGH THAT'S NEITHER HERE NOR THERE AT THE MOMENT.

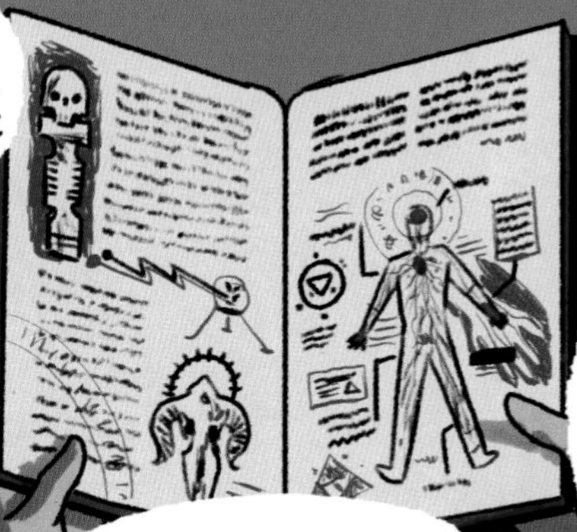

THIS IS THE SHADOW YOUR FATHER LIVED UNDER.

FURTHERMORE, ARTEMIS HAD LITTLE CAPACITY FOR PATERNAL BONDING, AND WHAT HE HAD IN THIS DEPARTMENT WAS DEVOTED ENTIRELY TO THE GOOD SON, HIS HONORED PUPIL, ELI.

ARTEMIS WAS VEHEMENTLY OPPOSED TO THE FACULTY'S FOUNDING.
TO HIM, THE ALLIANCE WASN'T SEEN AS ANYTHING OF THE SORT. HE SAW IT AS THE BLASPHEMERS TAKING OVER.
AN ACT OF HOSTILITY.
ALL THE WHILE, HE HAD ONE HELL OF A PRACTITIONER GROWING UP UNDER HIS VERY NOSE.
IT WASN'T UNTIL
NIGHT FRANCIS
TO LEAVE FOR BA
TRAINING THAT
TOLD ARTEMIS A
ELI THE TRUTH
ARTEMIS PRODUCED A SWORD FROM SEEMINGLY OUT OF NOWHERE AND TOLD YOUR FATHER HE WAS GOING TO CUT THE EVIL FROM HIM.
WHEN YOUR FATHER TOLD THAT PART OF HIS STORY, HE ALWAYS DID IT WITH A BIT OF A CHUCKLE, LIKE HE WAS JUST SHARING STORIES ABOUT HIS OLD MAN.
WHAT DID FRANCIS DO?

FLED. HE WAS ALREADY PACKED, HAD ASSUMED CORRECTLY WHAT ARTEMIS'S REACTION WOULD BE.
IT WAS ELI YOUR FATHER WAS REALLY TELLING.
ELI CAUGHT UP WITH FRANCIS AT THE TRAIN STATION JUST AS HE WAS ABOUT TO BOARD.
AT FIRST, YOUR FATHER'S HEART LEAPED. HIS BIG BROTHER WAS THERE TO SEE HIM OFF, ALL DIFFERENCES PUT ASIDE.
THAT WASN'T THE CASE, HOWEVER. ELI WAS SIMPLY THERE TO TELL YOUR FATHER NOT TO COME BACK. EVER. OR HE WOULD KILL HIM WITH HIS OWN HANDS.
THAT IS ELI MONTAGUE. THAT IS YOUR UNCLE.
AND THAT IS THE NEWEST MEMBER OF PORT HOWL'S FACULTY.

KNOCK
KNOCK
WHO IS IT?
IT'S PETE. CA
I COME IN?
YEAH,
IT'S OPEN.

QUITE A NIGHT.
REAL BEST-OF-TIMES, WORST-OF-TIMES THING GOING ON, HUH?
OUR BAND PLAYED IN FRONT OF PEOPLE. AND WE WEREN'T HALF BAD.
ONE OF MY FAVORITE ARTISTS IN MUSIC WAS THERE. HE LIKED IT.
THEN HE CAME TO HANG OUT WITH US.
I COULDN'T GET A SINGLE WORD TO HIM OUT OF MY MOUTH.
I THINK WE REALLY CONNECTED.
WE HAVE AN UNCLE.
HE'S PRETTY SCARY.
I PUNCHED A HOLE IN THE WALL.
YOU'RE PRETTY SCARY.
APPARENTLY, SO IS GRANDPA.
QUITE. A. NIGHT.

I LOVE YOU, MAN.
LOVE YOU TOO.
HEY, AL. DO YOU THINK I COULD BORROW THAT RECORD?
GIDEON'S BAND—WHAT WERE TH
CALLED?
GRAY HARBOR.
THANKS.
ROWAN'S TOMORROW?
BRIGHT AND EARLY.

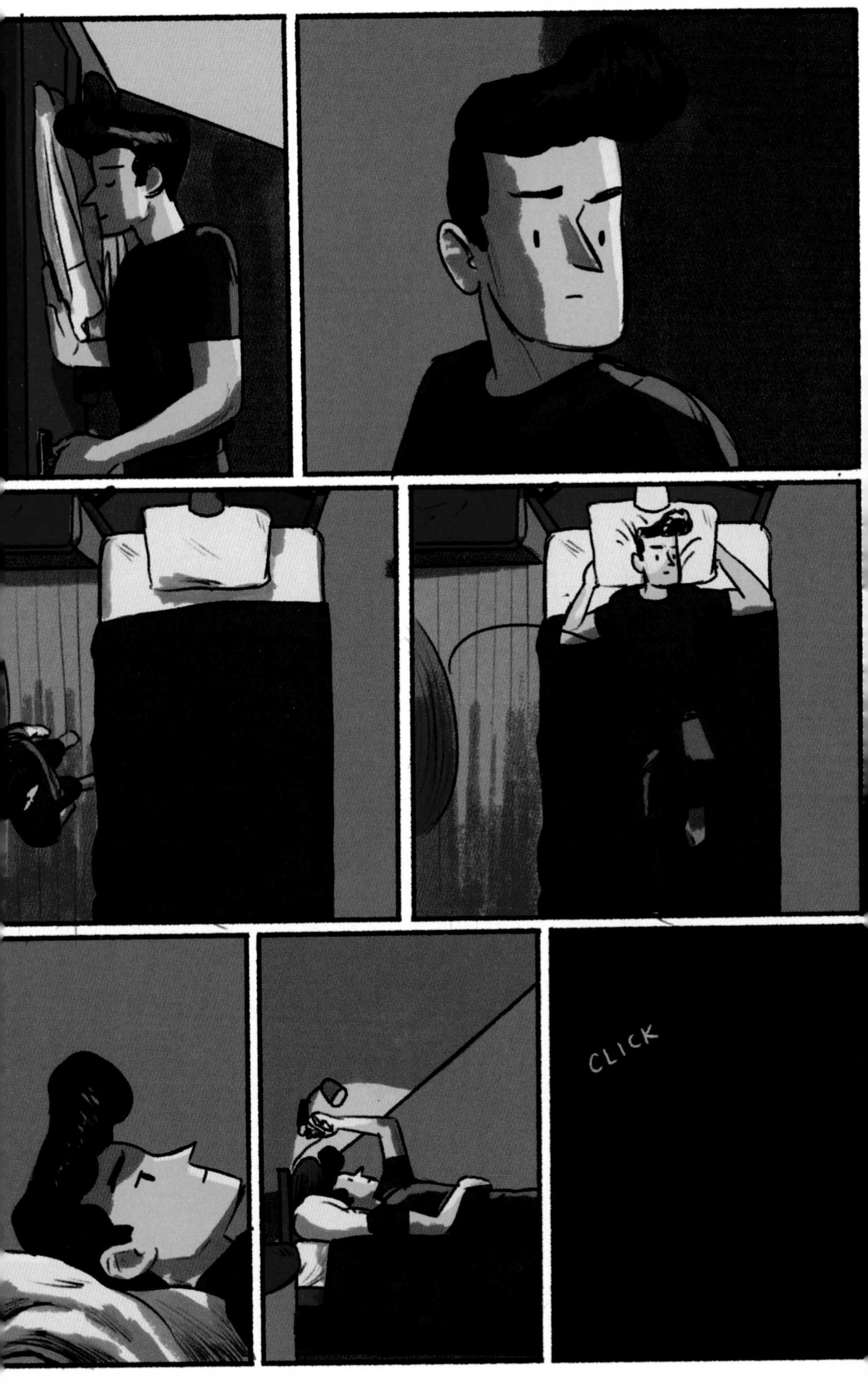
CLICK

CLICK
FUSION
JUNE 1968
GRAY HARBOR
Where The Devil Did They Come
BY:
ARLO BARRET

WHAT ARE YOU REALLY DOING IN PORT HOWL?

CHAPTER 3

HUH? WHAT?
KNOCK
KNOCK
YOU AWAKE? BROUGHT YO SOME COFFE

JUST A SECOND! I'M GETTING DRESSED.
GOOD MORNING, SUNSHINE.
IS IT?
YOU'RE LOOKING ROUGH. HOW ARE YOU FEELING?
ASK ME AFTER THE COFFEE.

RACHEL IS PICKING US UP IN FIFTEEN MINUTES.
YOU GOING TO MAKE IT?
DON'T YOU WORRY ABOUT ME. NOBODY LOVES SCHOOL ON A SATURDAY QUITE LIKE ALASTAIR S. MONTAGUE.
COME ON, IT'S NOT REALLY "SCHOOL." WE'RE LEARNING MAGIC.
YEAH, SPEAKING OF WHICH, I'VE GOT A FEW QUESTIONS FOR OUR TEACHER.

HOO BOY, THAT'S A STRONG BREW. CHUCK MAKE IT?
LIKE TAR, RIGHT?
I DIG IT.
HEY, PETE. CAN I TALK TO YOU ABOUT GIDEON?
I'M SO GLAD YOU BROUGHT HIM UP. I LISTENED TO GRAY HARBOR BEFORE I FELL ASLEEP LAST NIGHT AND AGAIN THIS MORNING.
WHY DIDN'T YOU TELL ME THEY WERE SO GOOD?
I DIDN'T THINK YOU WOULD BE INTO THEM.
WELL, I AM!
DO THEY HAVE ANYTHING ELSE?

JUST THE ONE ALBUM AND A COUPLE OF SINGLES WITH SOME PRETTY BOSS B SIDES. I'VE GOT THOSE TOO.
I HEARD HE PUT OUT A SOLO SINGLE THAT HE SOLD FOR ONE NIGHT ONLY AT A GIG IN BOSTON. IMPOSSIBLE TO FIND, THOUGH.
THAT'S SO WEIRD. DO YOU THINK IT WOULD BE RUDE TO ASK HIM ABOUT IT TODAY?
TODAY?
YEAH, WE'RE MEETING UP FOR LUNCH. HE SAID HE WANTED TO CHECK OUT FAT BLACK CAT DURING THE DAY. RACHEL AND CHARLIE ARE COMING.
WE INVITED YOU, BUT I GUESS YOU DON'T REMEMBER.
I REALLY DON'T.
AND NOW I'M GROUNDED. SO THAT'S COOL.

COME ON, FINISH YOUR COFFEE. WE HAVE TO GET GOING. ROWAN DOESN'T LIKE IT WHEN WE'RE LATE TO HIS LESSONS.
OH, YOU WANTED TO TALK TO ME ABOUT GIDEON?
YOU KNOW, I FORGET.
I'LL SEE YOU DOWNSTAIRS.

FRUITS & VEGETABLES
Merlin's Attic
SOLD
CLOSED
SOLD
KNOCK KNOCK
HOO BOY, DO WE HAVE SOME QUESTIONS FOR YOU.
GOOD MORNING TO YOU TOO, AL.
COFFEE'S ON. HELP YOURSELVES.

DON'T MIND IF I DO.
DAVID CALLED AHEAD TO LET ME KNOW YOU MIGHT HAVE SOME QUESTIONS, AL.
FROM HERE ON OUT, CONSIDER ME AN OPEN BOOK.
WHY ARE WE HAVING THESE LESSONS AND LEARNING THIS SHIT WHEN ALL IT SEEMS TO DO IS COMPLICATE THINGS?
DOES EVERYONE KNOW ABOUT MAGIC? BECAUSE IT SEEMS LIKE THIS BIG SECRET, YET EVERYONE WE COME ACROSS SEEMS TO HAVE SOMETHING TO DO WITH IT!

AND—
EASY, MAN, EASY.
HOW ABOUT WE TAK THEM ONE AT A TIME FROM THE TOP.
MAGIC IS COMPLICATED, SO THAT IT COMPLICATES THINGS IS SIMPLY ITS NATURE.
I KNOW THAT'S AN UNSATISFYING ANSWER, BUT LET ME SEE IF I CAN BREAK IT DOWN SOME MORE.
CHARLIE, WHAT DO YOU WANT TO DO WITH YOUR LIFE?
JESUS, YOU SURE YOU DON'T WANT TO ASK A MORE LOADED QUESTION?
HUMOR ME, PLEASE.

I'VE ALWAYS KINDA WANTED TO BE A JOURNALIST?
PERFECT! A JOURNALIST.
AND WHAT MAKES A GOOD JOURNALIST? I MEAN, BEYOND SOMEBODY WHO CAN WRITE WELL.
CLAP!
FAIRNESS, OBJECTIVITY, HONESTY . . . IN SHORT, SOMEONE WHO SEEKS TO FIND, AND COMMUNICATE, THE TRUTH.
NOW LET'S CONSIDER YOUR SPECIALTY. . . .
MY SPECIALTY?
YOUR ABILITY TO READ OBJECTS. OR, TO USE THE MORE TECHNICAL TERM, PSYCHOMETRY.
WOULD YOU NOT SAY THAT ABILITY COULD AID YOU IN THE FIELD OF JOURNALISM?
SURE.

ANOTHER EXAMPLE, ONE DAVID USED JUST YESTERDAY, IS THE PERSON ADEPT IN HEALING MAGIC TAKING UP MEDICINE. WHEN YOU ATTEND P.H.U. TO STUDY MAGIC, WHAT YOU'RE DOING IS SORT OF LIKE A DOUBLE MAJOR. IT'S NOT MEANT TO REPLACE A FIELD OF STUDY, BUT TO ENHANCE IT.
SO DO WE ALL HAVE SPECIALTIES?
I MEAN, IT'S LIKELY.
THERE ARE A FEW PRACTITIONERS WHO ARE MORE THE JACK-OF-ALL-TRADES SORT, BUT FOR THE MOST PART, THERE IS AN AREA EACH OF YOU WILL EXCEL IN.
A LARGE PART OF WHAT WE'RE DOING HERE IS TRYING TO FIND THAT OUT.
SO THERE WILL COME A TIME WHEN WE'RE ALLOWED TO USE MAGIC WHENEVER WE WANT?

YES, TECHNICALLY. ALTHOUGH, AS AL POINTED OUT, IT HAS A TENDENCY TO COMPLICATE THINGS MORE THAN HELP.

WHICH IS ANOTHER ELEMENT OF THIS EDUCATION: LEARNING THE HOW, AND THE WHEN, OF USING MAGIC.

ALL THIS TRACKING?

DOES THAT MEAN MARNIE AND LAUREL TOO?
AT FIRST, ALL WE COULD TALK ABOUT WAS THALIA AND THE NIGHT AT THE CEMETERY.
I THOUGHT IT WAS JUST THAT THEY DIDN'T WANT TO BRING IT UP AROUND THEIR BOYFRIENDS, WHO THEY ARE LITERALLY ALWAYS WITH NOW.
YES, THAT WOULD BE MY ASSUMPTION.
ASK THEM WHAT THEY REMEMBER ABOUT THAT NIGHT SOMETIME.
DO YOU HAVE SOMETHING TO CLEAN THAT UP WITH?
DON'T WORRY ABOUT IT, I'LL GET IT LATER.
BUT . . .

SO, HOW MANY PEOPLE LIKE US ARE THERE? LIKE YOU AND DAD?
PRACTITIONERS? WELL . . .
TO GIVE YOU SOME CONTEXT, THE LARGEST GRADUATING CLASS IN THE HISTORY OF PORT HOWL UNIVERSITY WITH A FOCUS IN MAGIC IS THREE.
SOMETIMES THERE WILL BE A STRETCH OF YEARS WHEN NOBODY IS ADMITTED.
I WAS THE LAST. AND YOU FOUR, HOPEFULLY, WILL BE THE NEXT.

THIS WAS MY ACCEPTANCE INTO PORT HOWL UNIVERSITY.
THERE'S NO NEED TO APPLY. YOU ARE SELECTED. OR YOU AREN'T.
NOW, ANY MORE QUESTIONS?
I HAVE AN ACTIVITY PLANNED.
JUST ONE . . .
WHAT HAPPENS NOW THAT THE FACULTY KNOWS? CAN WE STILL GET IN? WHAT ABOUT YOU AND DAVID?
I WAS HOPING IT WOULD BE AN EASY ONE.
WE ARE IN UNCHARTED TERRITORY HERE.
THIS SYSTEM, THE FACULTY, THE ALLIANC
IT'S ALL STILL RELATIVELY NEW.

IT WAS CREATED TO EASE THE MINDS OF THE INQUISITORS, WHO FEARED MAGIC WOULD RUN RAMPANT WITHOUT A PROPER SYSTEM IN PLACE.
NOW THE PRACTITIONERS ARE EAGER FOR SOME NEW BLOOD, WHICH WILL HELP US. . . .
BUT WE ALSO FLOUTED THE RULES RATHER EGREGIOUSLY.
I'M BEING HONEST WITH YOU WHEN I SAY I DON'T HAVE THE FIRST CLUE WHAT HAPPENS NEXT.
WE'RE EITHER OUT ON OUR ASSES AND POTENTIALLY ON TRIAL, OR YOU'RE ABOUT TO BECOME THE NEWEST MEMBERS OF A HIGHLY SECRETIVE MAGICAL FACTION.

NOW, IS THE QUESTION PERIOD OVER?
ACTUALLY, I WAS WONDERING—
I'M SORRY, THAT'S ON ME, I FRAMED THAT AS A QUESTION.
I WANT YOU EACH TO MAKE A PAPER AIRPLANE.
THAT'S IT?
WITHOUT TOUCHING THE PAPER.
THERE IT IS. . . .

BEGIN.

COME ON, AL,
YOU GOT THIS.
OTHING
APPENS
DAMN IT!

HOW DOES BEING ABLE TO FOLD AND FLY A PAPER PLANE HELP IF SOMEBODY HAS A GUN? OR IS USING MAGIC ON US?
DOINK
HEY!

HOW ABOUT THE ELEMENT OF SURPRISE?
TOUCHÉ.
LET'S CALL IT THERE FOR THE DAY.
AL, DAVID LET ME KNOW THAT I WAS TO BRING YOU STRAIGHT HOME TO WORK ON SOME REPAIRS.
ANYONE ELSE NEED A LIFT?

NO THANKS, WE'RE HANGING OUT AWHILE DOWNTOWN.
PSST. HEY.
WHY ARE YOU WHISPERING?
I NEED YOU TO DO A COUPLE OF THINGS FOR ME, OKAY?
WATCH GIDEON.
I THINK HE MIGHT BE INTO SOME REALLY DARK STUFF.
WHY ON EARTH WOULD YOU THINK THAT?
HIS IMAGE IS LITERALLY BUILT AROUND DARK STUFF. IT'S NOT A CRAZY STRETCH.

WAIT A MINUTE—I THOUGHT YOU LOVED HIM.
YES, OF COURSE I DO. THAT'S HOW I KNOW HE'S A FREAK.
IT'S ALL GOOD WHEN THE RUMORED DEVIL WORSHIPPER IS A POSTER IN YOUR LOCKER, KIND OF ANOTHER THING WHEN HE'S HANGING AROUND YOUR TWIN BROTHER.
LOOK, I SAW HIM TALKING TO TENNYSON LAST NIGHT, AND IT GOT PRETTY HEATED.
JUST ASK HIM ABOUT IT.
YOU'VE TALKED TO TENNYSON, RIGHT? IT CAN GET A LITTLE FRUSTRATING.
IT'S LIKE SPEAKING WITH THE CHESHIRE CAT.
FINE, WHAT ABOUT MILLIE?
WHAT ABOUT HER?
DID YOU SEE THE WAY SHE LOOKED AT HIM? TELL ME YOU BOTH SAW THAT.

LOOK, AL, I DON'T KNOW WHAT THE HELL IS GOING ON WITH YOU, BUT YOU'RE COMING OFF AS EXTREMELY JEALOUS, AND YOU KNOW WHAT? SELFISH.
THAT'S WITHOUT DRAGGING A SICK GIRL INTO WHATEVER FANTASY YOU'RE WEAVING.
JEALOUS? HOW? BY TRYING TO PROTECT MY BROTHER?
LOOK, WE GET YOU'RE UPSET T YOU CHOKED IN F OF ONE OF YOU HEROES. BUT NOB MADE YOU DRINK THE GODDAMN AND FREAK OU LAST NIGHT.
JUST BE HAPPY FOR PETE FOR A CHANGE.
CHUCK, IT'S NOT LIKE THAT—
FORGET IT, AL.
WHAT WAS THE OTHER THING?

YOU SAID THERE WERE A COUPLE OF THINGS.
HUH?
RECONNAISSANCE, AND WHAT WAS THE OTHER?
ANY PRINT THAT MENTIONS GIDEON, GRAY HARBOR, OR ANYTHING TO DO WITH MAGIC AND SATANISM.
CASH FOR THE MAGAZINES.
TELL TENNYSON IT'S FOR ME AND USE MY CREDIT.
I THOUGHT YOU SPENT THAT ON THE SHOW.
DAMN IT!
I DON'T HAVE ANYTHING ON ME.
YOU'RE PAYING ME BACK. PLUS MY LUNCH.
DEAL.

FIGURED I COULD FEED YOU BEFORE TAKING YOU BACK.
YES, PLEASE, I'M STARVING.
HOW'S THINGS?
YOU KNOW ME, MAN. I'M ALWAYS GOOD.

YOU LOOK HAGGARD, AL.
DIDN'T GET MUCH SLEEP.
WHY'S THAT?
IF THIS IS ABOUT THE PAPER PLANE THING, I'LL GET IT NEXT TIME.
IT'S NEVER YOUR ABILITY THAT I WORRY ABOUT, AL.
SOMETIMES I LOOK AT YOU AND IT'S LIKE YOU'RE A SKIPPING STONE SKITTERING OVER THE WATER.
NEVER SETTLING, BUT CAUSING A RIPPLE WHEREVER YOU LAND.
MAGIC OFTEN NEEDS TO BE ABOUT THOSE MOMENTS WHEN YOU'RE SETTLED.
OR, NOT EXACTLY. BECAUSE IT'S NOT LIKE QUICK THINKING DOESN'T HAVE ITS PURPOSE. OR THAT SLOW THINKING IS ALWAYS GOOD. I GUESS IT'S MORE LIKE AGILE THINKING.

DO YOU GET WHAT I'M TRYING TO SAY?
DO *YOU* EVEN KNOW WHAT YOU'RE TRYING TO SAY?
THEY CAN'T ALL BE WINNERS, OKAY?
HOW'S YOUR FIREBALL THESE DAYS?
IT'S COMING ALONG.

HEY, ROWAN?
DO YOU KNOW ABOUT OUR FAMILY? MY GRANDFATHER? ARTEMIS MONTAGUE?
I DO.
WHY DIDN'T YOU TELL US?
HONESTLY, AL? DIDN'T FEEL LIKE MY PLACE.

AND HOW ABOUT THE FACULTY? YOU COULDN'T HAVE SHARED THOSE DETAILS? MAYBE INSTEAD OF HAVING US MAKE PAPER AIRPLANES?

AL, ASK YOURSELF, DO YOU THINK ANYBODY IN YOUR LIFE ISN'T DOING THE BEST THEY CAN WITH THE INFORMATION THEY HAVE?

DAVID? SHELLY? ME?

PEOPLE ARE TRYING, MAN. BUT CAN I TELL YOU SOMETHING?

PART OF BECOMING AN ADULT IS REALIZING YOUR PARENTS, OLDER SIBLINGS, TEACHERS, NONE OF THEM KNOW SHIT.

THEY'RE JUST DOING THE BEST THEY CAN. NOBODY HITS IT OUT OF THE PARK EVERY AT BAT, YOU KNOW? THERE'S GOING TO BE SOME UGLY SWINGS.

WHAT MATTERS IS THAT YOU HAVE PEOPL YOU TRUST TO KEEP STEPPING UP TO THE PLATE FOR YOU.

SEE, THAT'S A BETTER METAPHOR. MARGINALLY.
WHAT WAS ALL THAT SKIPPING STONES SHIT?
THAT WAS A SWING AND A MISS.
LET'S GET YOU HOME.

IN ALL MY NINETEEN YEARS ON THIS PLANET, I HAVE NEVER, EVER HAD FRIES THAT GOOD.
SEE, TOLD YOU.
THERE WAS THIS ONE PLACE IN L.A. RIGHT AROUND THE CORNER FROM WHERE WE RECORDED THE ALBUM. THOSE FRIES COME PRETTY CLOSE, BUT I'LL GIVE THE EDGE TO JJ'S.
YOU MUST HAVE TOURED EVERYWHERE. SEEN EVERY CITY. WHAT WAS THAT LIKE?
ACTUALLY, NO. A LOT OF SHOWS HERE. A COUPLE IN CANADA. AND ONE IN EUROPE BEFORE I HAD TO COME BACK.

WHAT COULD HAVE POSSIBLY MADE YOU COME BACK FROM EUROPE? IT MUST HAVE BEEN SO BEAUTIFUL.
MY SISTER PASSED AWAY.
I'M SO SORRY, GIDEON, I—
NO, PLEASE. I MEAN, THANKS. OR YEAH, YOU DIDN'T KNOW.
I STILL HAVEN'T FIGURED OUT WHAT TO SAY WHEN SOMEONE SAYS "I'M SORRY," YOU KNOW?
I DO.
BELLLCHH
WE SHOULD GET A MOVE ON.

LUNCH IS ON ME.
PETER. CHARLIE. IT'S GOOD TO SEE YOU BOTH AGAIN.
PLEASURE TO MEET YOU, I'M ELI MONTAGUE.
LIKEWISE. I'M GIDEON.
WE WERE JUST LEAVING.

PETER, IF I MAY . . .
IT'S OKAY, GUYS. I'LL CATCH UP.
DID HE SAY "MONTAGUE"? DOES THAT MEAN . . .
LONG-LOST UNCLE. REAL BAD NEWS. I'LL FILL YOU IN LATER.
LISTEN, I'M SORRY FOR JUST DROPPING IN LIKE THAT. I . . . COULDN'T THINK OF A BETTER WAY.
YOU'RE GOING TO BE REALLY EXCITED WHEN I TELL YOU ALL ABOUT THIS NEW INVENTION CALLED THE TELEPHONE.
POINT TAKEN.
IF YOU'LL EXCUSE ME.
LISTEN TO ME A MINUTE. BY NOW I'M SURE DAVID HAS FILLED YOU IN ON EVERYTHING, EH?
WELL, JUST REMEMBER, THAT'S ONE SIDE OF THE STORY, AND THAT'S NOT EVEN COMING DIRECTLY FROM FRANCIS.
I DON'T HAVE ANY DOUBTS THAT DAVID MEANS WELL, BUT HE DOESN'T KNOW THE HALF OF IT, YOU HEAR?

GET YOUR HAND OFF OF ME.
LOOK. GIVE ME THE CHANCE TO TALK TO YOU AND YOUR BROTHER FACE TO FACE. JUST THE THREE OF US.
I REALLY DON'T SEE THAT HAPPENING.
WILL YOU AT LEAST RUN IT BY ALASTAIR?
YEAH, I'LL TELL HIM.
est 1947
HOME of the

YOU COMING IN?
NAH, NOT TODAY. I'M OUT OF
TOWN FOR THE NEXT FEW DAY
GOING TO VISIT MY FAMILY.
WHERE ARE THEY?
RHODE ISLAND.
WHAT'S THE MATTER, MAN?
WHAT IF SOMETHING HAPPENS WHEN YOU'RE GONE?
IT'S ONLY FOR A FEW DAYS. ANY
BETWEEN THE FOUR OF YOU, I T
YOU'VE SHOWN YOU DON'T NEED
FIGHTING YOUR BATTLES.
MAYBE, BUT I LIKE OUR CHANCES A LOT MORE.
TELL YOU WHAT . . .
HERE'S THE NUMBER AT MY PARENTS'.

THIS IS FOR THE IN-BETWEEN STUFF. OTHING SO SMALL YOU CAN'T FIGURE IT OUT OR YOURSELF, NOTHING O BIG YOU SHOULDN'T GO RIGHT TO SHELLY AND DAVID.
THANKS, ROWAN.
YOU SHOULD GET IN THERE.
ROWAN?
YEAH?
SHOULD WE BE SCARED OF THE FACULTY?
A FEW DAYS AGO, BEFORE I KNEW YOUR UNCLE WAS JOINING THE INQUISITORS' TABLE, I WOULD HAVE SAID PROBABLY.

AND NOW?
IF HALF OF WHAT I HEAR ABOUT ELI IS TRUE?
WE'RE ALL FUCKED.
COOL. GOOD NEWS.
HEY, I'LL BE BACK SOON. AND WE'LL GET THIS ALL FIGURED OUT.
GIVE YOUR FAMILY MY BEST.

GAZINES
WHAT ARE YOU DOING?
OW!
WHAT DID AL SAY TO YOU?
DID YOU JUST PINCH ME?
SERVES YOU RIGHT, LISTENING TO THAT BONEHEAD.
THAT *BONEHEAD* WAS BESIDE HIMSELF WHEN YOU LEFT. I'VE NEVER SEEN HIM LIKE THAT.
OH, WAS AL MAKING A SCENE? IMAGINE THAT!
OKAY, FAIR POINT. BUT IT WASN'T LIKE THAT.
LOOK, I GET YOU NOT WANTING ANYTHING TO DO WITH THIS ONE, GIVEN YOUR HISTORY WITH PETE.
SO I'LL DO IT.

RACHEL BRADFO
DO YOU HAVE
THING FOR AL?
HA HA HA HA HA HA!
I DON'T THINK SO.
THEN WHAT IS ALL OF THIS? YOU FLIRTING WITH HIM? GOING OFF AND TALKING TO HIM ON THE BEACH?
FLIRTING WITH HIM? ARE YOU SERIOUS?

I JUST RECOGNIZE SOMETHING IN HIM, ALL RIGHT?
OH, WHAT'S THAT?
HE'S IN PAIN, CHARLIE. AND FOR SOMEONE SO PERCEPTIVE, YOU SURE HAVEN'T CAUGHT ON TO THAT ONE, HAVE YOU?
SAY, TENNYSON.
WHA?
YOU SEE THAT GUY?
I DO.
WAIT. DO YOU SEE THAT GUY?
YOU WERE TALKING TO HIM LAST NIGHT. SEEMED LIKE IT GOT A LITTLE TENSE. WHAT WAS THAT ABOUT?

EARTH TO TENNYSON. COME IN, TENNYSON.
SORRY, WHAT WAS YOUR QUESTION?
OH, FOR THE LOVE OF . . .
THAT GUY, THE ONE BEHIND ME, THE ONE THAT WE BOTH SEE . . . YOU WERE TALKING TO HIM LAST NIGHT.
WHAT WAS THAT ABOUT?
RIGHT, RIGHT, RIGHT.
HE WAS ASKING ABOUT A SINGLE BY GIDEON DRAKE. APPARENTLY, HE CALLED LAST WEEK TO SEE IF IT WAS IN, IT WAS, NOW IT'S NOT.
HE GOT KIND OF RILED UP OVER IT. WANTED TO KNOW WH BOUGHT IT, AND I TOLD HIM TH WOULD BETRAY THE OATH.
WHAT OATH?
THE RECORD STORE OWNER OATH. ALL SALES ARE FINAL AND ALSO CONFIDENTIAL.
YOU MADE THAT UP.
I TAKE IT VERY SERIOUSLY.

THANK YOU, THIS HAS BEEN AN ABSOLUTE WASTE OF TIME.
Gideon Drake
HEY, THIS GUY LOOKS LIKE THAT GUY.
ASTUTE.
What Happened To Gideon Drake? Inside The SHOCKING Last Days of GREY HARBOR

GOOD AS NEW?
BETTER.
YOU KNOW, AL, IF YOU EVER NEED TO TALK . . .
I KNOW, SHELS.
I'LL HAVE TO GET STARTED ON THE PAINTING IN THE MORNING. THAT PATCH JOB WILL TAKE A WHILE TO SET.

ON AIR
KEEP

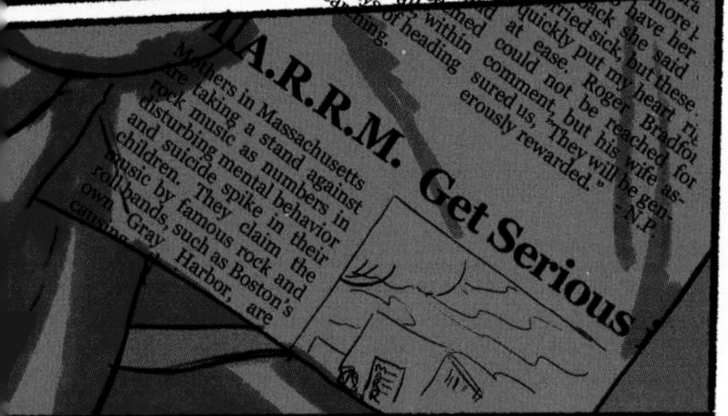
M.A.R.R.M. Get Serious
Mothers in Massachusetts are taking a stand against rock music as numbers in disturbing mental behavior and suicide spike in their children. They claim the music by famous rock and roll bands, such as Boston's own Gray Harbor, are causing
worried sick, but these quickly put my heart at ease. Roger Bradford could not be reached for comment, but his wife assured us, "They will be generously rewarded." -N.P.

"MOTHERS IN MASSACHUSETTS ARE TAKING A STAND AGAINST ROCK MUSIC AS INSTANCES OF DISTURBING MENTAL BEHAVIOR AND SUICIDE SPIKE IN THEIR CHILDREN."

SHELLY, DID YOU BUY A PAPER THE DAY THAT PETE AND I WERE IN IT?
OF COURSE, I GOT ONE AT THE STORE. I FIGURED YOU TWO WOULD WANT ONE AS WELL.
OH, SHELLY, YOU'RE THE BEST! WHERE IS IT? CAN I SEE IT?
OKAY, BUT YOU CAN'T CUT THIS ONE UP.

WHERE'S PETE?
"THANKS, RACHEL." "REALLY APPRECIATE IT, RACHEL." COME ON, MAN.
I'M SORRY, I JUST . . . I NEED TO TALK TO HIM.

HE WENT TO A MOVIE WITH GIDEON. *NIGHT OF THE LIVING DEAD.*
WHY DIDN'T YOU GO?
YOUR GIRL HERE IS NOT DOWN WITH HORROR MOVIES.
WHAT?
WHAT ABOUT YOUR WHOLE . . . YOU?
TREAD CAREFULLY, AL.
YES, I AM SOMETIMES DRAWN TO THE MACABRE, BUT HORROR MOVIES? NO WAY.

AND WHY DIDN'T YOU GO?
SEEN IT.
LOOK AT THIS.
THIS IS A NEW LEVEL OF VANITY, AL. GREETING YOUR GUESTS WITH NEWSPAPER ARTICLES YOU'RE FEATURED IN?
'Hot Dog' Teen Sleuths Find Missing Dog
NO, LOOK AT THIS.
M.A.R.R.M. Get Serious in Boston
"A SOUTH BOSTON MOTHER BELIEVES THAT ONE HARD-TO-FIND RECORD IN PARTICULAR IS TO BLAME FOR THE DEATH OF HER SON. THAT IS THE FIRST SOLO PRESSING BY GRAY HARBOR SINGER GIDEON DRAKE.
DRAKE'S SINGLE HAS GAINED A CERTAIN AMOUNT OF NOTORIETY FOR BEING AN ELUSIVE COLLECTOR'S EDITION. THIS RECORD, SHE SAYS, WAS THE LAST SONG HER SON PLAYED RIGHT BEFORE TAKING HIS OWN LIFE UPON RETURNING HOME FROM DRAKE'S ONE AND ONLY SOLO SHOW THAT NIGHT."

SHIT.
WHAT?
WELL, ON THE ONE HAND, THINK YOU SHOULD BE CARE ABOUT WHAT YOU READ IN THE PAPER.
DOES IT SAY IF IT WAS ORIGINALLY PUBLISHED SOMEWHERE ELSE?
HMM . . . THE *LEDGER.*
YEAH, THAT'S A RAG. THEY WILL, AND HAVE, PRINTED ANYTHING.
NEWSPAPERS CAN DO THAT?
TRUE JOURNALISM IS HARDER TO COME BY THAN YOU MIGHT THINK.
THAT SAID . . .
AND I NEED YOU TO STAY RATIONAL, OKAY?
I SPOKE TO TENNYSON.

the AERO
NIGHT OF THE LIVING DEAD
7:00
THE AERO
I CAN'T BELIEVE YOU HAVEN'T SEEN THIS YET.
TO BE HONEST, I DON'T GET OUT TO THE MOVIES OFTEN.

Night OF THE LIVING DEAD

WELL? WHAT DID HE SAY?
HE SAID THAT GIDEON WAS UPSET THERE WASN'T A COPY OF HIS SINGLE IN THE STORE.
APPARENTLY, HE CALLED AHEAD LAST WEEK TO MAKE SURE, NOW HERE HE IS.
COME ON, YOU GUYS!
NONE OF THIS IS STRANGE TO YOU?
HERE'S WHAT I WILL SAY.
I DON'T BLAME YOU FOR HAVING QUESTIONS.
AND SHE'S BACK! THANK YOU, CHUCK.

BUT, AL, BUDDY, YOU'RE ALL OVER THE PLACE.
I JUST DON'T THINK IT'S AS SINISTER AS YOU'RE MAKING IT OUT TO BE.
I'VE SPENT TIME WITH HIM. IF I THOUGHT PETE WERE IN ANY DANGER, WOULD I BE HERE RIGHT NOW?
MILLIE!
WE HAVE TO FOLLOW UP WITH MILLIE.
BECAUSE WE'RE GOOD PEOPLE AND WANT TO MAKE SURE SHE'S DOING BETTER, RIGHT?
NOT BECAUSE YOU WANT TO QUESTION HER
OF COURSE NOT.
IN THAT CASE, I WAS GOING TO SEE HOW SHE WAS ANYWAY. BUT I'M NOT GOING UNTIL TOMORROW.
SO, IN THE MEANTIME, BE A DEAR AND TURN ON THE TV, THE SATURDAY MOVIE IS STARTING SOON.

NIGHT OF THE LIVING DEAD 7:00
SO? WHAT DID YOU THINK?
HONESTLY? SCARIER THAN I WAS EXPECTING.
BUT REALLY GOOD!
DO YOU MIND IF WE KEEP WALKING FOR A BIT? I LOVE THIS WEATHER.
SURE.
ALL RIGHT, WHERE ARE WE HEADED?
DON'T TELL ME THE MOVIE SPOOKED YOU. . . .
OF COURSE NOT.
COME ON. I'M GOING TO SHOW YOU MY FAVORITE TREE.

WHAT ARE YOU REALLY DOING IN PORT HOWL, GIDEON DRAKE?

UM, JUST HERE TO GET AWAY FROM IT ALL. WORK ON MY ALBUM. YOU KNOW, KIND OF PULL A DYLAN AND DISAPPEAR FOR A WHILE.

BULLSHIT.
YEAH. I GUESS IT IS.
CARE TO TRY AGAIN?
LOOK, PETE. I . . .
I AM REALLY ENJOYING SPENDING TIME WITH YOU. A LOT.
BUT . . .
I'M A DANGEROUS PERSON TO BE AROUND, PETE.

R. ROCK STAR, HEARTBREAKER. ROUPIE IN EVERY TOWN.
NO, IT'S NOT LIKE THAT.
THEN WHAT IS IT LIKE?
YOU WOULDN'T BELIEVE ME IF I TOLD YOU.
I THINK YOU'D BE SURPRISED BY THE THINGS I BELIEVE.
LET'S GET YOU HOME.

"What Happened to
Gray Harbor?"
Bandmates Notice
change in
Lyrics to new
made specific reference
to DEMONS

DO YOU HAVE ANY IDEA WHAT TIME IT IS?
LITTLE AFTER TEN?
IT'S TEN-THIRTY-TWO P.M.
AL, IS THIS A JOKE? YOU'RE ON MY CASE FOR GOING TO SEE A MOVIE?
I DON'T THINK YOU SHOULD BE HANGING OUT WITH GIDEON.
ARE YOU SERIOUS? THE ONLY REASON I EVEN KNOW WHO HE IS IS BECAUSE OF YOU.
THOUGHT HE YOUR FAVORITE MUSICIAN.
HE WAS.
OR, HE IS.
I JUST . . . I THINK HE'S BAD NEWS. I'VE BEEN LOOKING INTO HIM A BIT MORE—
YOU'VE BEEN LOOKING INTO HIM?
JESUS, AL, YOU COULD HAVE BEEN HANGING OUT WITH US IF YOU HADN'T GOTTEN YOURSELF GROUNDED.

IT'S NOT ABOUT THAT.
I THINK HE MIGHT BE DANGEROUS, PETE. EVERYTHING I READ TELLS ME HE'S INTO SOME REALLY DARK STUFF.
HE MIGHT EVEN BE TO BLAME FOR THE DEATH OF A GUY IN BOSTON.
STOP! JUST STOP! LISTEN TO YOURSELF, AL.
HE'S INTO SOME DARK STUFF?
PEOPLE ARE ENTITLED T THEIR DEMONS.
NO SHIT, SO ARE WE!
INTERESTING CHOICE OF WORDS.
DOES THIS HAVE ANYTHING TO DO WITH GIDEON? OR IS THIS JUST ABOUT YOU HAVING YOUR EGO HURT?
I WAS WORRIED ABOUT YOU.
I'M TRYING TO PROTECT YOU.
NO, YOU'RE TRYIN TO CONTROL ME. ARE ALWAYS TRYING CONTROL ME.
I'M GOING TO BED.

LET'S WATCH THE REST OF THE MOVIE.
CAN SOMEONE TELL ME WHAT I MISSED?
WHAT PART DID YOU FALL ASLEEP AT?
THE BEGINNING.

CHAPTER 4

NBC
WBQN
5
WHAT THE—
WHAT THE HELL IS WRONG WITH YOU? ARE YOU TRYING TO SCARE ME TO DEATH?
I NEED YOU TO TAKE ME TO BOSTON.

WHAT DO YOU HAVE ALL OVER YOU?
PAINT.
RACH, CAN YOU TAKE ME TO BOSTON OR NOT?
IT'S GOT TO BE NOW, BEFORE EVERY WAKES UP.
NO. WHAT IS THIS ALL ABOUT?
I THINK THERE MIGHT BE SOMETHING SERIOUSLY WRONG WITH GIDEON.
AL, I THINK YOU NEED TO LET THIS GO.
I UNDER-STAND, RACH.
DO ME A FAVOR DON'T TELL ANY WE TALKED.

AL! ALASTAIR, YOU GET BACK HERE WHEN I'M TALKING TO YOU.
I'VE GOT TO FIND OUT, RACHEL.
WHY?
BECAUSE IF I'M RIGHT, HE'S GOING TO HURT SOMEBODY. AND THE WAY THINGS ARE SHAPING UP, IT LOOKS LIKE THAT SOMEBODY IS GOING TO BE PETE.
NOT ON MY WATCH.
LOOK AT ME!
WHAT IS GOING ON WITH YOU?
WHY ARE YOU ALL OVER THIS GUY? WHY IS IT SO HARD TO TRUST THAT HE'S JUST KIND OF INTO YOUR BROTHER? PETE'S NOT UNATTRACTIVE, YOU KNOW.
BECAUSE I DON'T TRUST *ANYBODY*!

PEOPLE LIE. PEOPLE DISAPPEAR WITHOUT A TRACE. PEOPLE SHOW UP OUT OF NOWHERE. PEOPLE ONLY TELL YOU WHAT'S CONVENIENT FOR THEM, AND THAT'S ONLY WHEN THEY ABSOLUTELY HAVE TO.
EVERYONE IS SO FULL OF SHIT ALL THE TIME. WELL, THAT' FINE, BECAUSE YOU KNOW WHAT I GOOD AT? FINDING SHIT OUT. AN THAT'S WHAT I INTEND TO DO.
YOU SHOULD GET BACK INSIDE. IT' FREEZING OUT.
HOW DO YOU PLAN ON GETTING THERE?
BUS.
THEY WON'T SELL A TICKET TO A MINOR.
I'LL HITCHHIKE.
GREAT, AND YOU WIND UP DEAD IN A DITCH TWENTY MINUTES OUTSIDE PROVIDENCE.
THEN WHAT DO YOU SUGGEST I DO?
GO INSIDE. WASH SOME OF THIS PAINT OFF.
THEN WE'LL GO.

WET PAINT
GONE SLEUTHIN'
BACK SOON
WITH LOVE
A
WELL, THIS SHOULD BE GOOD.

WE'RE ALMOST THERE. WHERE'S OUR FIRST STOP?
RICH CAUFIELD, THE GUITARIST OF GRAY HARBOR, SAID THAT WITH THE BAND BROKEN UP, HE WAS GOING BACK TO THE BAR HE USED TO WORK AT.
AND IN AN INTERVIE FROM ALMOST TW YEARS AGO, HE TAL ABOUT HOW HE USE TO WORK AT A PLA CALLED . . . THE BELL IN HAND.
TERRIFIC. WE'RE JUST TWO UNDERAGE KIDS PULLING UP TO A BAR EARLY ON A SUNDAY. NOTHING SUSPICIOUS THERE.
ASSUMING THIS RICH GUY IS EVEN WORKING, WHAT THEN?
WE ASK HIM TO POINT US IN THE DIRECTION OF THIS JOURNALIST, ARLO. HE'S WRITTEN SEVEN STORIES ON GRAY HARBOR AND GIDEON IN THE LAST TWO YEARS.
PRETTY SHAKY PLAN TO GET GROUNDED TILL THE SEVENTIES FOR. YOU SURE ABOUT THIS?
IF WE TURN AROUND RIGHT NOW, WE MIGHT BE ABLE TO GET BACK BEFORE ANYONE NOTICES YOU'RE GONE.
BOSTON
26 MILES
I'M SURE.

HAVE YOU BEEN TO BOSTON?
NO, NEVER HAD THE CHANCE. YOU?
I USED TO COME INTO THE CITY ALL THE TIME WITH MY MOTHER.
HEY, WE HAVE A FEW HOURS UNTIL THE BAR OPENS, RIGHT?
I'M GOING TO TAKE YOU SOMEWHERE.
IT'S CLOSE TO WHERE WE'RE GOING.

SO NEITHER OF YOU HAS ANY IDEA WHERE HE MIGHT HAVE GONE?
WHAT CASE WAS HE WORKING?
NOT A CASE EXACTLY.
SPILL IT.
HE'S BEEN INVESTIGATING GIDEON DRAKE.
GIDEON DRAKE? WHY DO I KNOW THAT NAME?

HE'S A MUSICIAN. ONE OF AL'S FAVORITES.
THAT THE ONE HE'S ALWAYS GOT COMING FROM HIS ROOM? GREAT BARBER?
GRAY HARBOR.
WHATEVER.
TELL ME AL ISN'T STALKING THIS MAN.
NO, IT'S NOT LIKE THAT.
THEN WHY THE SUDDEN INTEREST?
IT'S ACTUALLY A FUNNY STORY. GIDEON IS STAYING IN TOWN. HE SAW US PLAY THE OTHER NIGHT. ONE THING LED TO ANOTHER, AND NOW WE'RE . . . I DON'T KNOW, FRIENDS WITH HIM?
SO AL IS INVESTIGATING A FRIEND OF YOURS?
KIND OF, YES.
WHY?

I THINK IT'S BECAUSE HE AND I HAVE BECOME VERY CLOSE. GIDEON, I MEAN.
I'M STILL NOT UNDERSTANDING.
GIDEON AND I . . .
LIKE EACH OTHER.
A LOT.

YES, I GET IT, YOU'RE FRIENDS WITH GIDEON. I STILL DON'T KNOW WHY AL WOULD BE SO TROUBLED BY—
NO, DEAR. I THINK WHAT PETE IS TRYING TO SAY IS THAT HE AND GIDEON HAVE A MUCH STRONGER CONNECTION THAN THAT.
WELL, OF COURSE.
I MEAN, HE WOULD HAVE TO BE A FOOL NOT TO BE ENCHANTED BY YOU.

AND THIS IS AL . . .
TRYING TO LOOK OUT FOR ME. I THINK. I MEAN . . . AT FIRST I THOUGHT HE WAS JUST MAYBE JEALOUS?
NOW I THINK HE MIGHT ACTUALLY BE AFRAID.
AND WHAT MIGHT YOU HAVE TO FEAR FROM GIDEON DRAKE?
WHY IS AL SO CONCERNED?
HE'S AFRAID PETE'S NEW BOYFRIEND IS A SATAN WORSHIPPER.
CHANNELING DEMONS AND SUCH.
JUST THREW THAT RIGHT OUT THERE, HUH?
IS HE?
I DON'T THINK SO? I MEAN, SOME OF HIS MUSIC GETS A BIT DARK, SURE. AND OKAY, HE DOES HAVE A PENCHANT FOR OCCULT JEWELRY. AND HE MIGHT HAVE MENTIONED LAST NIGHT THAT HE WAS DANGEROUS TO BE AROUND.
THERE'S A CHANCE HE MIGHT WORSHIP THE DEVIL, I'M REALIZING THAT NOW.

PETE, HOW WOULD YOU FEEL ABOUT US MEETING GIDEON? PERHAPS HE CAN COME BY FOR LUNCH?
SURE? I MEAN . . YOU WANT TO MEE HIM?
YES, I BELIEVE I DO.
AND, PETE, I APOLOGIZE IN ADVANCE IF EMBARRASS YOU, BUT I MUST DO WHAT FATHERS DO WHEN THEIR KIDS START DAT
I'M GOING TO ASK THIS YOUNG MAN IF HE WORSHIPS THE DEVIL.

YOU SURE DO LOVE A CEMETERY, DON'T YOU?
GUILTY.
BUT THAT'S NOT MY FAVORITE PART OF THIS PLACE.
OH? YOU MEAN THERE'S SOMETHING MORE RACHEL BRADFORD THAN THIS?
DO WHAT?
DON'T DO THAT.
START THINKING YOU KNOW EVERYTHING ABOUT ME.

DO YOU THINK ABOUT THEM A LOT? YOUR PARENTS?
I USED TO.
I MEAN, I STILL DO
IT'S JUST NOT WIT
THAT SHARP PAIN ARO
THE EDGES, YOU KNO
IT'S WHY PETE AND I STARTED THE DETECTIVE THING. WE THOUGHT WE MIGHT BE ABLE TO FIND THEM. OR FIND OUT WHAT HAPPENED TO THEM.
AND THE REST WAS HISTORY.
DID YOU EVER FIND ANYTHING?

COME ON, WE WERE JUST IDIOT KIDS. WHAT WERE WE REALLY GOING TO DO?
WELL, YOU'RE NOT IDIOT KIDS ANYMORE. IDIOTS, MAYBE. BUT NOT KIDS. YOU EVER THINK ABOUT TRYING AGAIN, NOW THAT YOU'RE OLDER? KNOW A BIT MORE?
I'M A ONE-MYSTERY-AT-A-TIME KIND OF GUY.
WHAT ABOUT YOU? YOU THINK ABOUT YOURS A LOT?
YEAH. FOR OPPOSITE REASONS.
MY FATHER? WELL, OU MET MY FATHER. HE COMES UP WHENEVER I FALL INTO A SPIRAL.
SPIRAL?

YEAH, LIKE . . . THIS CYCLONE OF NEGATIVE THOUGHTS THAT PICKS ME UP, CARRIES ME AWAY, THEN BRINGS A HOUSE DOWN ON MY HEAD LIKE I'M THE FUCKING WICKED WITCH OF THE EAST.
IT'S HIS VOICE I HEAR TELLING ME I'M AWFUL.
AND WHAT ABOUT WHEN YOU THINK OF HER?
I GO HERE.
HERE?
OVER THERE, DURING THE SUMMER, THERE ARE THESE BOATS. BIG SWAN BOATS THAT HAVE TO BE PEDALED.
MY MOM WOULD ALWAYS BRING ME HERE WHEN THINGS GOT REALLY BAD.
WE SHOULD COME BACK. IN THE SUMMER. TAKE A RIDE.
YEAH. WE SHOULD.

HELLO?
HI. HEY. GIDEON?
PETE.
SO, UM, I WAS WONDERING, WOULD YOU AYBE WANT TO COME HERE R LUNCH TODAY? DAVID ND SHELLY WOULD REALLY LIKE TO MEET YOU.
GIDEON?

NO, PETE. I DON'T WANT TO DO THAT.
I'M SORRY, I JUST THOUGHT . . .
IT'S NOT A GOOD IDEA. NOT TODAY.
BUT MAYBE ANOTHER DAY?
I DON'T
PETE.
DO YOU STILL WANT TO SEE ME TODAY?
SURE. WHY DON'T YOU COME BY HERE?
MAYBE AROUND TWO?
SURE. SURE, SOUNDS GOOD.
I'LL SEE YOU THEN.

WAS THAT GIDEON? WHAT TIME IS HE COMING?
HE'S NOT.
NOT A GOOD DAY?
NO, HE SAID ANOTHER TIME FOR SURE. HE HAS A LOT TO DO.
I SAID I MIGHT GO OVER THERE FOR A BIT, IF THAT'S OKAY?
PETE, I'M NOT SURE THAT'S A GREAT IDEA. TH AL SO WORKED UP, IT JUST SEEMS . . . I THINK DAVID AND I SHOULD GET TO KNOW HIM.
WHAT IF THERE IS SOMETHING OFF ABOUT HIM? AND WE JUST LET YOU GO OVER THERE ALONE?
PLEASE, SHELLY?
YOU FINISH PUTTING AWAY THE GROCERIES. I'LL GO TALK TO DAVID.

WELL?
MRS. LEFEBVRE, HI. I'M HERE TO SEE MILLIE?

MILLICENT UNABLE TO ME TO THE DOOR.
MRS. LEFEBVRE, MY FRIENDS AND I, WE ARE THE ONES WHO FOUND MILLIE—ER, MILLICENT—ON THE BEACH.
I WANTED TO SEE HOW SHE'S DOING.
SHE'S FINE.
IF YOU MUST KNOW, MILLICENT'S AILMENT WAS BROUGHT ON BY A SPIRITUAL LAPSE.
I'M NOT SURE IF I FOLLOW. SHE LOOKED . . .
SHE LOOKED LIKE A GIRL WHO DANCED WITH SIN AND SHOULD BE GRATEFUL HER CONSEQUENCES WERE NOT MORE SEVERE.
HOW ABOUT YOU, GIRL? DO YOU INVITE SIN INTO YOUR HOME?
OF COURSE YOU DO. I CAN PRACTICALLY SMELL IT ON YOU.
PERFORMING ROCK MUSIC. FRATERNIZING WITH THE OTHER MORAL DELINQUENTS AROUND TOWN.

AND YOUR PARENTS—
WHAT'S THAT ABOUT MY FAMILY?
SUFFICE IT TO SAY THE PROVERBIAL APPLE DOESN'T FALL FAR FROM THE TREE.
PLEASE GIVE MILLIE OUR BEST.
YOU STAY AWAY FROM MY DAUGHTER.
THAT GOES FOR YOU AND ALL YOUR FRIENDS!
SLAM!

NOT YOUR FIRST UNAUTHORIZED EXIT, I SEE.
SHH. THE BITCH HAS EARS LIKE A BAT.
COME WITH ME.

THAT'S HIM.
MORNING. WHAT'LL IT BE?
I'M GOOD. FIND ALCOHOL DOESN'T AGREE WITH ME.
I'M DRIVING.

NO, I'VE JUST HAD A FEW PEOPLE LIKE YOURSELVES COME IN TO TALK TO ME ABOUT GRAY HARBOR.

SO WHICH IS IT? WHY DID WE REALLY BREAK UP? ARE WE GETTING BACK TOGETHER? IS THERE ANY MORE MUSIC COMING?

THERE'S MAYBE A COUPLE OF SONGS ON SOME MASTER TAPES SOMEWHERE THAT AREN'T WORTH THE STRAIN ON YOUR EARS.

WELL, YOU'D HAVE TO TALK TO GIDEON ABOUT THAT.
AND WHY DID YOU BREAK UP?
FUNNY YOU OULD MENTION HIM.
HE ROLLED UP TO OUR TOWN A COUPLE OF DAYS AGO.
AND WHERE'S THAT?
PORT HOWL.
PORT HOWL? WHAT THE HELL S GIDEON DOING THERE?
WELL, RICH, THAT'S KIND OF WHAT WE WERE HOPING YOU COULD TELL US.
SEEMS HE AND MY BROTHER HAVE REALLY HIT IT OFF.
I GREW UP WITH GIDEON. I'M TWO YEARS OLDER, SO I WAS MORE FRIENDS WITH HIS BIG SISTER, AUTUMN.
HE WAS ALWAYS A LITTLE OUT THERE, BUT ALL THAT DARK SHIT? IT WAS JUST AN ACT. AN IMAGE.
THEN AUTUMN PASSED, AND I DON'T KNOW, HE STARTED BECOMING MORE AND MORE LIKE THE CHARACTER GIDEON, LESS LIKE THE GIDEON I KNEW.

HIS SISTER WAS ALL HE HAD.
THEIR MOTHER IS A REAL JESUS FREAK. THREW GIDEON OUT WHEN HE WAS FIFTEEN.
AUTUMN HAD HER OWN PLACE WITH HER BOYFRIEND, AND THEY TOOK GIDEON IN.
HOW DID SHE GO?
CANCER.
NOW HE'S JUST GOT THIS BLACK CLOUD HANGING OVER HIM ALL THE TIME. AND HIS MUSIC— SONGS HE WAS BRINGING TO THE BAND—IT WAS . . . DARK.
I MEAN, WE ALREADY HAD PEOPLE PROTESTING OUR SHOWS, YOU KNOW? MOTHERS AGAINST ROCK-AND-ROLL MUSIC? THEY WERE THERE EVERY NIGHT. SAYING WE WERE A DANGER TO THEIR CHILDREN.
BULLSHIT, RIGHT?
I DON'T KNOW. WAS IT BULLSHIT?

THINGS STARTED HAPPENING.
WHAT HAPPENED, RICH?
WHEN HE PLAYED HIS NEW SONG FOR US, IT WAS ONLY HALF DONE. JUST A GUITAR LICK AND A BIT OF HUMMING. BUT I . . . I WENT SOMEWHERE.
NO, I WAS TAKEN. . . .
I KNEW THAT WHENEVER HE FINISHED THAT SONG, IT WAS GOING TO BE THE MOST BEAUTIFUL THING I'D EVER HEARD.
I ALSO KNEW IT MIGHT JUST KILL ME. AND I MEAN THAT. I DON'T KNOW HOW, BUT I MEAN THAT.
IF THE ANGELS HAVE MUSIC, GIDEON'S IS THE EXACT OPPOSITE.
I THINK YOU BEST DO EVERYTHING YOU CAN TO GET YOUR BROTHER AWAY FROM HIM.

HI THERE.
HELLO YOURSELF.
HI, MRS. NORMANDY.
SHE SEEMS NICE.
THIS IS HER HOU
I'M JUST RENTI
THE MAIN FLOC
POOR GI
CAN'T HEA
THING.

LEAVE YOUR SHOES ON, I NEED TO CLEAN THE FLOORS ANYWAY.
I'M NOT GOING TO LIE, YOUR PLACE IS . . . COZIER THAN I WOULD HAVE EXPECTED.
WELL, I'M NOT SURE HOW LONG I'LL BE RENTING.
NO SENSE IN SENDING FOR MY COFFIN JUST YET, YOU KNOW?
HAR HAR.
WOULD YOU LIKE A COFFEE?
MAYBE SOME WATER, PLEASE.
I SEE YOU BROUGHT YOUR GUITAR.
YEAH. I WAS HOPING I COULD PLAY YOU A SONG I'VE BEEN WORKING ON.
I'VE HAD THE MUSIC FOR A WHILE, BUT THE LYRICS JUST CAME TO ME.
OH, IS THIS A WORLD PREMIERE?

YOU MIGHT SAY.
WELL, DON'T I JUST HAVE THE LUCK OF THE DEVIL?
SO JUST KEEP IN MIND, I'M NOT A PROFESSIONAL. AND IT'S A WORK IN PROGRESS. BUT . . . UM . . .
PETE, IT'S OKAY. PLAY YOUR SONG.
HERE GOES . . .
NEVER STOPPED SO LONG TO ASK . . . WHAT IT IS I'M LOOKING FOR.
ALWAYS MOVED FROM TASK TO TAS
BEEN AFRAID OF WANTING MORE
DO YOU THINK THAT YOU MIGHT STAY? OR BE GONE LONG BEFORE?

YOU'RE GONNA GIVE ME THE CHANCE TO SAY YOU'RE THE ONE THAT I ADORE.
WHEN I SAW YOU, SWEET HARMONY . . .
WHEN I SAW YOU, YOUR MELODY . . .
I CAN'T STOP YOU . . .
FROM DESTROYING ME . . .
BUT WOULD I IF I COULD?
OH, WOULD I IF I COULD?

LOOK, GUYS, THE BAR IS STARTING TO FILL UP. IS THERE ANYTHING ELSE I CAN HELP YOU WITH?
DO YOU KNOW HOW WE CAN GET A HOLD OF THIS MAN?
Journalist
ARLO BARRETT
ARLO?
I DON'T MAKE A HABIT OUT OF MEMORIZING MUSIC JOURNALISTS' HOME ADDRESSES.
BUT I GOT HIS PHONE NUMBER. YOU CAN CALL THE OPERATOR FOR THE ADDRESS.
THAT WILL DO JUST FINE, THANKS. THEN WE'LL GET OUT OF YOUR HAIR.

OKAY, STAY ON BROADWAY AND TURN ONTO AMES, THEN GO LEFT ONTO MAIN.
WELL. HOW ARE YOU DOING AFTER THAT CONVERSATION?
NOT GREAT.
SCREEEECH!!
WHAT THE HELL, RACH, ARE YOU TRYING TO GIVE ME WHIPLASH?
DIVERSION
MAYBE WE SHOULD TALK TO THEM?
MOTHERS AGAINST ROCK & ROLL MUSIC

AL, I THINK YOU SHOULD STAY IN THE CAR.
HA!
NO, NO, NO. THIS DETECTIVE SHIT IS KIND OF MY BAG.
TAKE A LOOK AT YOURSELF AND TELL ME IF YOU THINK YOU LOOK THE PART OF WHAT THESE WOMEN WOULD DEEM TO BE AN UPSTANDING YOUNG MAN.
YOU ALSO DESPERATELY NEED TO BRUSH YOUR TEETH.
NOW, THIS YOUNG LADY, ON THE OTHER HAND, MIGHT JUST GET THEM TO TALK WITHOUT PROSELYTIZING.
POSTAL-A-WHAT?
JUST STAY IN THE GODDAMN CAR AND KEEP YOUR HEAD DOWN.
HH HH HH.
RECORDS

MILLIE, WHAT'S GOING ON? WHERE ARE WE GOING?
ARE YOU OKAY?
I'M NOT SURE HOW TO ANSWER THAT.
I'M BETTER THAN I WAS THE OTHER NIGHT.
WELL, I'M GLAD TO HEAR THAT.
I'M STILL NOT SURE WHERE WE'RE GOING. . . .
THERE.

OH, GOOD. I WAS WORRIED IT WAS GOING TO BE SOMEPLACE CREEPY.
OKAY, SO I LIKE THIS GUY, BILLY THORPE—HE GOES TO SAINT JAMES, SO YOU PROBABLY DON'T REALLY KNOW HIM.
SOMETIMES WE COME OUT HERE WITH A FEW OTHER KIDS FROM CHURCH, AND WE HANG OUT, DRINK WARM BEER, AND TALK ABOUT WHAT TOTAL ASSHOLES OUR PARENTS ARE.
BILLY WOULD ALWAYS BRING HIS RECORD PLAYER AND SOME RECORDS HE MANAGED TO STEAL FROM FAT BLACK CAT.
ALWAYS ROCK. HEAVY STUFF. GUITARS THAT JUST GO FROM CRUNCHY TO SCREECHY. "DEVIL'S MUSIC," MY MOM CALLS IT. I HAD NEVER HEARD IT BEFORE BILLY. WAS NEVER ALLOWED.

ONE TIME, BILLY BRINGS THIS RECORD, AND HE LOOKS AT ALL OF US SO SERIOUS, AND HE GOES, "THIS RECORD CHANGED MY LIFE."
WE ALL JUST KINDA LAUGHED AT HIM. BILLY IS REALLY FUNNY.
BUT HE DIDN'T LAUGH WHEN WE DID. HE JUST WENT ABOUT PUTTING ON THE RECORD.
WE ALL SAT THERE, LISTENING.
IT WAS THE FIRST TIME WE HAD EVER JUST LISTENED TO A SONG TOGETHER, YOU KNOW?
USUALLY IT WAS BACKGROUND NOISE FOR OUR FLIRTING.
I DIDN'T MIND THE STUFF HE USUALLY PLAYED, BUT I ALSO DIDN'T LOVE IT.
THIS I LOVED.
THEY WEREN'T SONGS, THEY WERE MOVEMENTS, YOU KNOW?
THE WORDS WEREN'T LYRICS, THEY WERE LIKE . . . LIKE . . .

SPELLS?
YEAH. YEAH! LIKE SPELLS.
BILLY MUST HAVE SEEN IT ON MY FACE, BECAUSE THE NEXT TIME WE ALL HUNG OUT, HE BROUGHT THIS NEW SINGLE FROM THE SINGER.
NOT THE BAND, JUST HIM.
HE GAVE IT TO ME AND ASKED IF I WANTED TO COME TO THE CABIN ALONE WITH HIM THE NEXT NIGHT TO LISTEN TO IT.
HE HADN'T EVEN HEARD IT YET, HE WANTED TO WAIT FOR ME.
BILLY IS THE SWEETEST.
YOU DIDN'T WAIT UNTIL THAT NIGHT, THOUGH, DID YOU, MILLIE?

I DID, BUT BILLY NEVER CAME.
SO I PUT IT ON BY MYSELF. . . .
WHAT WAS THE NAME OF THE BAND, MILLIE? WHO WAS THE SINGER?
GRAY HARBOR.
THE SINGER'S NAME IS GIDEON DRAKE.

GIDEON, SAY ANYTHING.
PETE, I THINK YOU SHOULD LEAVE.
I'M SORRY. I JUST . . .
THAT WAS DUMB, WASN'T IT?
I SHOULDN'T HAVE PLAYED YOU THAT.
WHAT DO YOU WANT FROM ME, PETE?
WHAT, DID YOU THINK THIS WAS GOING TO BE SOME SORT OF FAIRY TALE? I'D LISTEN TO YOUR SONG AND, WHAT, PUT YOU IN TOUCH WITH A LABEL?
IS THAT WHAT THIS IS ABOUT? YOU THINK I'M TRYING TO USE YOU FOR YOUR CONNECTIONS?
I JUST WANTED TO PLAY THE SONG I WROTE.
FOR YOU.

I DON'T KNOW WHAT YOU WANT FROM ME, PETE, BUT WHATEVER IT IS, IT'S NOT GOING TO HAPPEN.
MEETING YOUR FAMILY? LISTENING TO YOUR STUPID SONG?
I DIDN'T COME HERE FOR THIS PUPPY-DOG-LOVE BULLSHIT, ALL RIGHT?
I CLEARLY MISREAD THIS WHOLE SITUATION. I THOUGHT YOU LIKED ME.
I DON'T THINK THAT GIVES YOU THE RIGHT TO BE SO FUCKING CRUEL.
WELL, IT DIDN'T SEEM LIKE YOU WERE GETTING THE HINT.
I HATE THAT AL WAS RIGHT ABOUT YOU.

AND HOW ABOUT YOU, DEAR? HAVE YOU SUCCUMBED TO THE PROFANE INSTILLATION OF ROCK AND ROLL?

NO, MA'AM. IN FACT, I JUST SAW YOUR SIGNS AND WANTED TO STOP AND LEND MY SUPPORT.

THAT'S A NICE NAME. BIBLICAL, ISN'T IT?

SOMETHING LIKE THAT.

AND WILL YOU TAKE UP THE MANTLE, THALIA?

OH, SHOOT, DON'T YOU KNOW I WOULD, BUT I DO NEED TO BE GETTING BACK TO PORT HOWL BEFORE TOO LONG.

I WAS JUST IN TOWN TO ATTEND A LOVELY SERVICE AT PARK STREET CHURCH.

SAY, YOU KNOW, I WAS HOPING YOU LADIES MIGHT HAVE SOME ADVICE FOR ME.
TURNS OUT, WE'VE GOT THIS ROCKER WHO JUST ROLLED UP TO PORT HOWL. I WOULDN'T LIKE HIM ON A GOOD DAY, BUT THIS ONE, THERE'S SOMETHING ABOUT HIM THAT SCARES ME.
YOU'RE QUITE RIGHT TO FEEL THAT WAY.
MIGHT WE ASK THIS MISCREANT'S NAME?
GIDEON DRAKE.
SWEET THALIA, IF YOU HAD SAID ANY OTHER NAME, I MIGHT HAVE TOLD YOU PORT HOWL CAN TAKE CARE OF ITSELF.
GIDEON DRAKE, THOUGH? HE IS THE VERY EMBODIMENT OF EVIL.
THAT BAD?

PURE AND SIMPLE.
HE'S CONSPIRED WITH THE DEVIL TO ENSNARE ALL THOSE WHO LISTEN TO HIS MUSIC FOR PLEASURE.
HAVE YOU LISTENED TO IT?
OH YES. ONE MUST KNOW WHAT IT IS THEY FIGHT AGAINST.
WE CHASED HIM STRAIGHT OUT OF BOSTON. I'M ONLY SORRY TO HEAR IT WAS RIGHT TO YOUR DOORSTEP.
THAT'S WHAT HE DOES, YOU KNOW. HE GOES TOWN TO TOWN, PLANTING HIS SONG, INFECTING THE CHILDREN. THEN POOR, UNSUSPECTING YOUNG PEOPLE LISTEN TO IT, AND BEFORE YOU KNOW IT, THEY . . . THEY . . .
MOTHERS AGAINST
YES?
THEY CHANGE, POOR THINGS. A SICKNESS THAT STARTS IN THE SOUL AND MANIFESTS IN THE BODY.
THEY STOP TALKING. STOP EATING. SOME DIE, CONSUMED BY THE EVIL.
AND BEFORE YOU SAY YOU DON'T BELIEVE IT, MY NEPHEW SAW HIM AT A CONCERT, TOOK HOME A RECORD, AND DIDN'T EVEN MAKE IT THROUGH THE NIGHT.

WE HAD LOST HIM TO SIN LONG BEFORE THAT, BUT WE HOPED HE MIGHT STILL BE SAVED.
ONLY ONE THING THAT CAN DO THAT.
DEVIL'S MUSIC.
THE DEVIL' MUSIC.
AL.
AL, GET UP.
HUH? WHERE AM I?
WELL, I'M GLAD SOMEBODY IS CATCHING UP ON THEIR SLEEP.
DID YOU FIND ANYTHING OUT?
YES. IT SEEMS THAT FOR THE FIRST TIME EVER, YOU AND THE CHRISTIAN RIGHT ARE ON THE SAME PAGE.
OH, I'M GOING TO NEED YOU TO ELABORATE ON THAT.

I'LL EXPLAIN ON THE WAY TO ARLO'S.
·2·5·11·14·
RAMBLER
Before I be your dog to get you
here
FOR LEASE
I'll make you walk alone; baby please don't go,
Baby, please don't go...
Baby, please don't go...
YOU'LL BURN IN HELLFIRE!
BABY PLEASE DON'T GO – THE BEACON STREET UNION

AHHHHHHHH!!!!

CORONER
WHAT HAPPENED HERE? ARLO BARRETT?
OH, YOU KNEW HIM?
HE WAS JUST—
MY UNCLE.
MA'AM, I'M SORRY, YOU MIGHT WANT TO SIT DOWN.
JUST TELL ME HOW IT HAPPENED.
I REALLY SHOULDN'T SAY UNTIL WE KNOW MORE.
PLEASE?
ACCIDENTAL OVERDOSE, LOOKS LIKE.
AGAIN, I'M VERY SORRY, MA'AM.

MY FIANCÉ AND I WERE JUST COMING TO VISIT HIM.
DO YOU THINK . . . THERE'S ANY WAY WE COULD GO INSIDE? SEE HIS PLACE ONE LAST TIME?
Mirror, mirror,
On the wall...
Guess I'm my father's
Son after all.
RACHEL.

WHAT ARE WE EVEN LOOKING FOR?
WHY DON'T YOU TAKE A LOOK THROUGH SOME OF THESE NOTEBOOKS. LOOK FOR ANYTHING ABOUT GIDEON.
I'LL CHECK OUT THE REST OF THE APARTMENT.

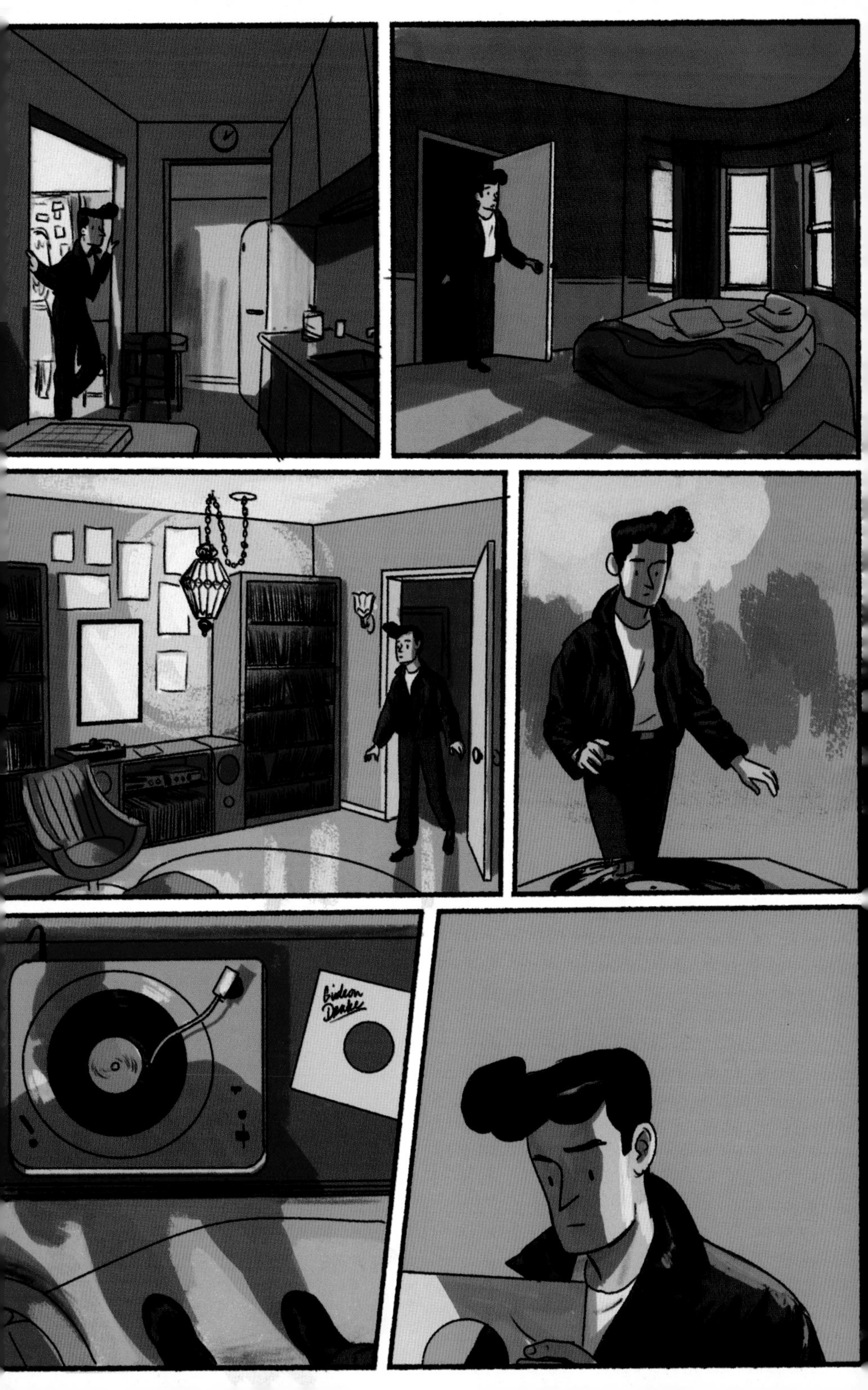
Gideon
Drake

HEY, AL, I THINK I MIGHT HAVE SOMETHING!
AL?

CHAPTER 5

BANG!
BANG!

OH, HI, RACH—
THAT'S RIGHT, I'M A WITCH, MOTHERFUCKER. SO WHATEVER FREAKY SHIT YOU'RE UP TO DOESN'T SCARE ME.
WHAT—HOW DID YOU . . . ? WHAT THE HELL WAS THAT?

NOW YOU TELL ME HOW TO FIX IT, OR I'LL REARRANGE YOUR FINGERS.
FIX WHAT? I HAVE NO IDEA WHAT YOU'RE TALKING ABOUT. . . .
A WITCH?
FIX WHAT?!

HI, MRS. NORMANDY!
HIM.
BRING HIM INSIDE.
WE NEED TO TALK, AND HE SHOULDN'T BE ALONE.
NO TALKING.
JUST.
FIX.
HIM.
I DON'T KNOW HOW!
PLEASE, JUST LET ME EXPLAIN.

START TALKING.
HAVE YOU EVER FELT SO ALONE . . .
SO COMPLETELY ALONE, AND AFRAID OF HOW ALONE YOU ARE,
THAT YOU LOOK FOR ANYTHING TO JUST TAKE THAT PAIN AWAY, IF ONLY FOR A MOMENT?
ONE MOMENT OF PEACE FROM YOUR OWN GODDAMN NIGHTMARE OF A BRAIN?
THAT WAS MUSIC FOR ME.
MY WAY OUT.

AS EVERYTHING FELL APART AROUND ME, I HAD MY MUSIC, AND I HAD HER.
I HAD AUTUMN. MY SISTER.
SHE TAUGHT ME EVERYTHING. HOW TO S HOW TO PLAY. HOW T FEEL AND EXPRESS TH MUSIC, NOT FROM ME BUT OF ME.
SHE WAS INCREDIBLE. BETTER THAN I WILL EVER BE.

THIS IS ALL SUPER FASCINATING, BUT I'M NOT SEEING HOW IT IS RELEVANT TO OUR CURRENT SITUATION.
ALL RIGHT, NO BULLSHIT.
AFTER SHE DIED, I WANTED TO DIE.
IT WAS ALL I COULD THINK ABOUT. THIS NEVER-CEASING INTRUSIVE THOUGHT, AN EARWORM, A SONG YOU HEAR EVERY MINUTE, DAY IN, DAY OUT, REGARDLESS OF WHAT YOU'RE DOING.
I HAD A PLAN.
I WOULD RELEASE ONE LAST ALBUM. ALL MY OWN SONGS. I WOULD LAY MYSELF BARE IN THE HOPES THAT PEOPLE WOULD UNDERSTAND.
AND THAT SHE WOULD UNDERSTAND, IF SHE COULD STILL SEE ME.
IT STARTED WITH A SONG.
I RECORDED AND MASTERED IT MYSELF.
OF COURSE, I CRAVE THE SPOTLIGHT.
LEO.
SAGITTARIUS.
NO SHIT.

SO I BOOKED A SHOW AND SOLD THE SINGLE.
THOUGHT IT WOULD BE LIKE THE BEGINNING OF THE END, YOU KNOW? A FAREWELL OF SORTS.
HARDLY ANYBODY SHOWED UP. MAYBE FIFTY PEOPLE IN TOTAL.
MOST OF THEM JUST WANTED GR HARBOR SONGS.
FIFTEEN PEOPLE BOUGHT THE SINGLE. BY MY COUNT, THIRTY-ONE PEOPLE HAVE BEEN AFFLICTED BY IT. I DON'T KNOW HOW MANY, BUT SOME HAVE DIED.
I'M TRYING TO STOP IT. FIND EVERY COPY AND DESTROY IT. BEFORE IT CAN DO ANY MORE HARM.
I'VE TAKEN CARE OF THREE, AND I THOUGHT I'D TRACKED ONE TO PORT HOWL, BUT I HAVEN'T BEEN ABLE TO FIND IT.

THIRTY-TWO.
NO, PLEASE, DON'T LET IT BE PETE. PLEASE TELL ME IT WASN'T PETE.
IT WASN'T PETE.
A MUSIC JOURNALIST. ARLO BARRETT.
ARLO. HE WAS A GOOD GUY. HE DIDN'T DESERVE THAT.
HOW?
OVERDOSE.

THIS IS WHAT IT DOES.
EVERYTHING I FELT WHILE MAKING IT IS PASSED ON TO THE LISTENER. THE DESPAIR, THE GRIEF, THE SELF-LOATHING.
MY MOTHER ALWAYS SAID SOMETHING ABOUT ME WAS WRONG.
SHE NEVER CALLED ME EVIL, NOT EXACTLY, BUT THE MEANING WAS THERE.
SO WHEN I STARTED MAKING MUSIC, I LEANED INTO IT. "YOU WANT EVIL? I'LL SHOW YOU EVIL."
IT WAS AN IMAGE. AT LEAST, THAT'S WHAT I THOUGHT.
AT LEAST, THAT'S WHAT I TOLD MYSELF.
THE THING IS, THOUGH, I ALWAYS KIND OF BELIEVED HER. IN THE BACK OF MY MIND, I KNEW SHE WAS RIGHT.
THE ONE THING THAT MAKES ME ANY GOOD, MY MUSIC, MIGHT JUST FUCKING KILL YOU IF YOU HEAR IT.
HOW'S THAT FOR CURSED?
TELL ME YOU DESTROYED THE RECORD?

BRADFORD

NO.
I CAME AS CLOSE TO IT AS I EVER WANT TO BE.
I DIDN'T TOUCH IT.
IT'S MY MESS. I'LL CLEAN IT UP.
SO A WITCH, HUH? WELL, I GUESS THAT CHECKS OUT.
TOO?
ALL OF US, BABY. PETE AND AL TOO.
THE BOY'S GOT SECRETS.

YOU DON'T HAPPEN TO KNOW WHAT *I* AM, DO YOU?
WHATEVER YOU ARE, I DON'T THINK IT'S EVIL.
I'VE LIVED WITH EVIL.
I KNOW SOME PEOPLE THAT I THINK YOU SHOULD MEET. YOU'VE CLEARLY GOT SOMETHING MAGICAL ABOUT YOU. I THINK THEY COULD HELP.

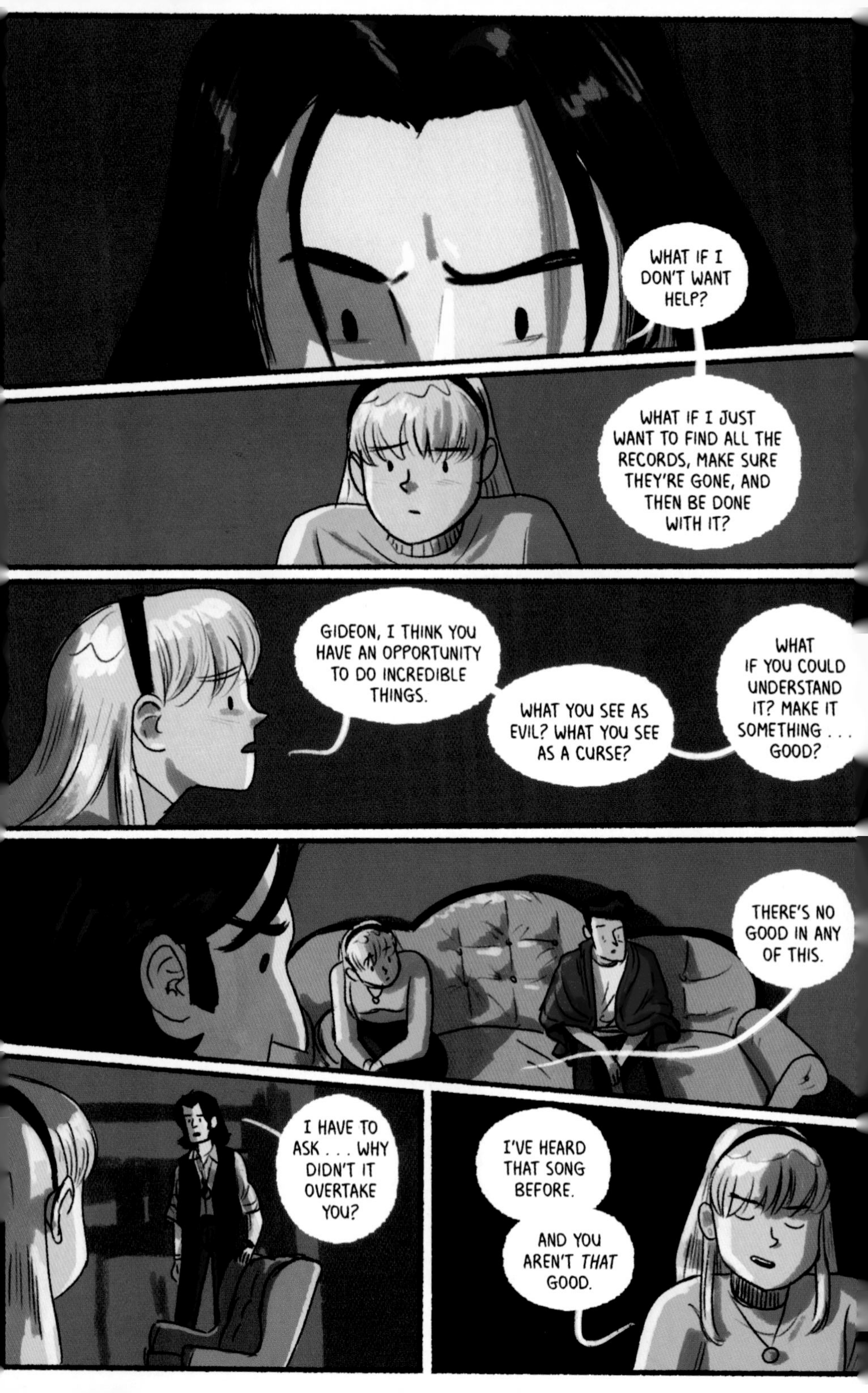
WHAT IF I DON'T WANT HELP?
WHAT IF I JUST WANT TO FIND ALL THE RECORDS, MAKE SURE THEY'RE GONE, AND THEN BE DONE WITH IT?
GIDEON, I THINK YOU HAVE AN OPPORTUNITY TO DO INCREDIBLE THINGS.
WHAT YOU SEE AS EVIL? WHAT YOU SEE AS A CURSE?
WHAT IF YOU COULD UNDERSTAND IT? MAKE IT SOMETHING . . . GOOD?
THERE'S NO GOOD IN ANY OF THIS.
I HAVE TO ASK . . . WHY DIDN'T IT OVERTAKE YOU?
I'VE HEARD THAT SONG BEFORE.
AND YOU AREN'T *THAT* GOOD.

AERO
AERO

TORONTO
WHITBY
OWEN SOUND
COLLINGWOOD
BARRIE
ORANGEVILLE
GUELPH
GODERICH
STRATFORD
BRANTFORD
WOODSTOCK
ONTARIO
SYRACUSE
ROCHESTER
WATERTOWN
TICONDEROGA
ALBANY
AUBURN
BINGHAMTON
HARTFORD
CONCORD
PORTSMOUTH
BOSTON
Cape Cod
PROVINCETOWN
NEW BEDFORD
THE
AERO
ADMIT ONE
NOW LEAVIN
PORT HO
"Come back so

FROM WHAT ALL OF YOU TOLD ME, I AM CONFIDENT SAYING THAT IT'S AN ENCHANTMENT.
A POWERFUL ONE. BUT JUST AN ENCHANTMENT. IT WILL DISSIPATE. NO DEVILS OR DEMONS.
AND IT'S POSSIBLE GIDEON CAST IT WITHOUT EVEN KNOWING?
MUSIC IS A POWERFUL MAGIC ALL ITS OWN. IT'S A CONDUIT AND A CONDUCTOR OF EMOTIONAL ENERGY.
IN A WAY, EVERY SONG IS LIKE A SPELL, YOU UNDERSTAND?

I'VE READ ABOUT A FEW CASES OF THIS. "GLOOMY SUNDAY," ALSO KNOWN AS "THE HUNGARIAN SUICIDE SONG," BEING THE MOST NOTABLE.

IN THAT INSTANCE, HOWEVER, IT WASN'T JUST THE SONG. FAMINE, POVERTY, WAR, THEY WERE ALL CONTRIBUTING FACTORS TO A HIGH RATE OF MENTAL ILLNESS.

THE SONG ONLY AMPLIFIED THE DESPAIR THAT ALREADY EXISTED. IT GAVE IT A VOICE.

THANK GOODNESS MILLIE IS ALL RIGHT. THAT BODES WELL FOR US.
WE NEVER SHOULD HAVE BEEN THERE.
I'M SO, SO SORRY. DO YOU THINK PETE WILL EVER FORGIVE ME?
I THINK YOU KNOW AL WELL ENOUGH BY NOW TO KNOW THAT HE WAS GOING, WITH OR WITHOUT YOU. IF YOU HADN'T BEEN THERE?
I DON'T WANT TO THINK OF THAT.
HOW LONG DO YOU THINK IT WILL LAST?

IT'S HARD TO SAY. MAYBE A DAY OR TWO FOR THE WORST OF IT. MAYBE A WEEK BEFORE IT'S CLEARED UP ENTIRELY.

BUT I WANT TO REITERATE, THIS STATE HE'S IN? THOSE FEELINGS WERE ALREADY THERE. I DON'T BELIEVE THE SONG CREATED THEM.

WE'LL NEED TO KEEP A CLOSE EYE ON HIM. I'LL CLEAR MY SCHEDULE FOR THE WEEK TO BE AVAILABLE.

YOU KNOW I'M HERE WHENEVER YOU NEED ME, DAVID.

I KNOW.

THANK YOU FOR COMING BACK HERE SO QUICKLY. I'M JUST SORRY YOUR TIME WITH YOUR FAMILY WAS CUT SHORT.

HOW DID YOU KNOW TO COME BACK?

I GOT YOUR BACKS.

HEY.
THEY SAY YOU'RE GOING TO BE OKAY.
CREEM
GRAY HARBOR
ZIGZAG
AND IN CASE YOU NEEDED A BIT OF EXT
MOTIVATION, TURNS O
YOU WERE RIGHT ABO
EVERYTHING.
I WON'T PRETEND TO UNDERSTAND WHAT YOU ARE GOING THROUGH RIGHT NOW, AL, BUT JUST KNOW THAT YOU ARE SO LOVED.
PLEASE DON'T LEAVE ME.
PLEASE DON'T LEAVE ME.

HE'S NOT THERE.
AH, MRS. NORMANDY. GOOD EVENING.
I DON'T KNOW ABOUT THESE KIDS TODAY.
THEY GALLIVANT AROUND WITH WHOMEVER, WITH THEIR HAIR DOWN TO WHEREVER, SOME OF THEM GIRLS. IT'S EVEN UNDER THEIR ARMS.
YOU KNOW WHAT I THINK IT IS?
IT'S THAT MUSIC THEY LISTEN TO.
MARK MY WORDS, IT'S THAT MUSIC.
MIGHT BE, MRS. NORMANDY.
MIGHT JUST BE.

TICKETS
ONE WEEK LATER

CAN I COME IN?
SURE.
HOW YOU DOING TODAY?
BETTER THAN YESTERDAY. PROBABLY NOT AS GOOD AS TOMORROW.
THAT'S GOOD TO HEAR. VERY GOOD.
I REALLY APPRECIATE YOU CHECKING ON ME LIKE YOU HAVE BEEN, DAVE. I THINK I'M THROUGH THE WORST OF IT.
THAT'S VERY GOOD TO HEAR.

YEAH, YOU ALREADY SAID THAT.
I DID, DIDN'T I?
THE WARDROBE
C. S. LEWIS
I CAN'T BELIEVE IT.
WHAT? IT'S A GOOD BOOK.
OH, I KNOW VERY WELL HOW GOOD IT IS.
THAT'S NOT WHAT I'M LAUGHING AT.

OF ALL THE BOOKS N THIS HOUSE, YOU CHOOSE THAT ONE TO READ NOW.
YOUR FATHER GAVE ME THIS COPY.
AL, I AM SO SORRY TO BE RUDE, BUT GIVE ME JUST A MOMENT. I'D LIKE TO SHOW YOU SOMETHING.

AL, I'M GOING TO ASK YOU SOMETHING VERY PERSONAL. NOW, IF YOU DON'T WANT TO ANSWER IT, I'LL UNDERSTAND.
HOW DO YOU REMEMBER YOUR FATHER?
HE WAS A GOOFBALL.
MOM WOULD BE TRYING TO GET US TO BED, AND HE WOULDN'T WANT TO STOP READING TO US. WE NEVER HAD TO ASK FOR FIVE MORE MINUTES, IT WAS ALWAYS HIM.
HE DID A GREAT DAFFY DUCK. AN OKAY BUGS. AND JUST A GOD-AWFUL PORKY PIG.
HE WAS A GOOFBALL, WASN'T HE?
WHAT A LIGHT THEY BOTH WERE.
BUT ONE THING I REMEMBER VERY WE ABOUT YOUR FATHE SOMETHING YOU M NOT . . . IS HIS DA MOODS.

I GUESS . . . I REMEMBER DAYS WHEN THEIR BEDROOM DOOR WOULD BE SHUT.
HE WOULD ONLY COME OUT TO GRAB SOMETHING FROM THE KITCHEN.
MOM WOULD SAY DAD WASN'T FEELING WELL AND WE NEEDED TO LET HIM REST.
BEFORE YOU WERE BORN, HE WOULD DO THE SAME THING.
HE WOULD JUST DISAPPEAR. NOBODY WOULD HEAR FROM HIM FOR WEEKS.
ONE DAY I CONFRONTED HIM ABOUT IT.
IT HURTS, YOU KNOW? TO HAVE SOMEBODY WALK IN AND OUT OF YOUR LIFE.
TO ONE DAY BE SO PRESENT AND ENGAGING, THEN THE NEXT, JUST GONE.
SO I ASKED HIM, "FRANCIS, WHAT THE HELL IS GOING ON WITH YOU?"

WE GOT INTO A FIGHT. HUGE BLOWOUT. I TOLD HIM HE WAS A SELFISH PRICK. HE THREW SOME CHOICE WORDS MY WAY.
AFTER A FEW MINUTES, FRANCIS STORMED OUT AND I WAS LEFT SHAKING, INDIGNANT.
IT WAS ANOTHER MONTH OR SO BY THE TIME I HEARD FROM HIM AGAIN, AND IT WAS IN THE FORM OF A SMALL PACKAGE AND A LETTER.
WOULD YOU LIKE TO READ IT?
YOU HA
ON TO T

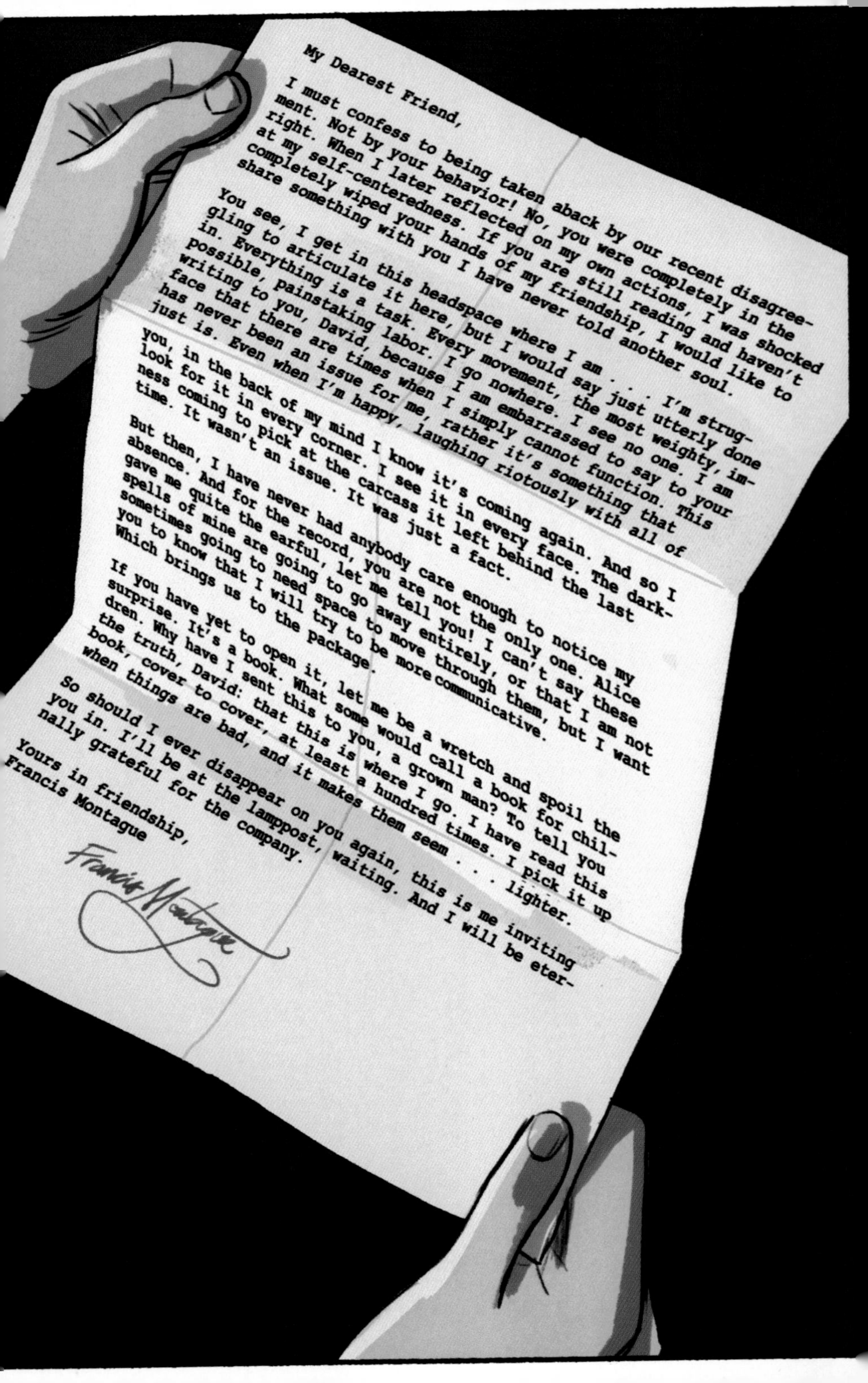

My Dearest Friend,

I must confess to being taken aback by our recent disagreement. Not by your behavior! No, you were completely in the right. When I later reflected on my own actions, I was shocked at my self-centeredness. If you are still reading and haven't completely wiped your hands of my friendship, I would like to share something with you I have never told another soul.

You see, I get in this headspace where I am . . . I'm struggling to articulate it here, but I would say just utterly done in. Everything is a task. Every movement, the most weighty, impossible, painstaking labor. I go nowhere. I see no one. I am writing to you, David, because I am embarrassed to say to your face that there are times when I simply cannot function. This has never been an issue for me, rather it's something that just is. Even when I'm happy, laughing riotously with all of you, in the back of my mind I know it's coming again. And so I look for it in every corner. I see it in every face. The darkness coming to pick at the carcass it left behind the last time. It wasn't an issue. It was just a fact.

But then, I have never had anybody care enough to notice my absence. And for the record, you are not the only one. Alice gave me quite the earful, let me tell you! I can't say these spells of mine are going to go away entirely, or that I am not sometimes going to need space to move through them, but I want you to know that I will try to be more communicative. Which brings us to the package.

If you have yet to open it, let me be a wretch and spoil the surprise. It's a book. What some would call a book for children. Why have I sent this to you, a grown man? To tell you the truth, David: that this is where I go. I have read this book, cover to cover, at least a hundred times. I pick it up when things are bad, and it makes them seem . . . lighter.

So should I ever disappear on you again, this is me inviting you in. I'll be at the lamppost, waiting. And I will be eternally grateful for the company.

Yours in friendship,
Francis Montague

Francis Montague

GOOD BOY.
HOW YOU FEELING? YOU WANT TO HEAD BACK?
NO. IT'S GOOD TO BE OUTSIDE.
YOU SEEM BETTER TODAY.
EVERY DAY GETS EASIER.
DO YOU WANT TO TALK ABOUT IT?

I DON'T KNOW THAT I'M THERE YET.
YOU WANT TO TRY?
NO. I LIKE WATCHING YOU TWO DO IT.
DO YOU EVER THINK ABOUT THEM?
MOM AND DAD? SURE. ALL THE TIME.
DO YOU REMEMBER WHEN WE WERE KIDS? JUST AFTER THEY LEFT?

WE STARTED THE DETECTIVE THING.
BECAUSE WE WANTED TO FIND THEM.
YEAH, I REMEMBER.
WHAT MA YOU THINK THAT?
WE'RE NOT KIDS ANYMORE, PETE.
NO, I GUESS WE'RE NOT.
WE SHOULD BE LOOKING FOR ANSWERS.
WE KNOW THINGS NOW.
YOU WANT TO DO THAT?
WHEN I'M BETTER. YEAH.
THEN THAT'S WHAT WE'LL DO.

LAST NIGHT BEFORE IT'S GONE FOR ANOTHER YEAR.
WHAT DO YOU SAY WE SHUT IT DOWN IN STYLE?
I DON'T THINK SO.
TELL YOU WHAT . . .
IF YOU CAN THROW THIS BALL TO CHAMP, THE INVISIBLE GHOST DOG, AND SOMEHOW NOT SMILE WHEN HE BRINGS IT BACK TO YOU, YOU DON'T HAVE TO GO.
BUT IF YOU SO MUCH AS CRACK THE SLIGHTEST, MOST MINUTE GRIN, YOU HAVE TO COME OUT.

HARRM

COME ON. YOU STILL OWE ME LUNCH, BUT I WILL ACCEPT PAYMENT IN THE FORM OF COTTON CANDY.

DING!

I KINDA MISSED THAT.
RACHEL, I JUST WANT TO SAY . . .
YEAH?

BEFORE I HAD ONE OF THE WORST DAYS OF MY LIFE, I THINK I WAS HAVING ONE OF THE BEST.
HOO BOY, IS THAT EVER A GOOD LINE!

OH, COME ON, WE HAVE TO GO!
THINK YOU CAN CATCH ME, OLD BOY?
CHALLENGE ACCEPTED.

DO YOU WANT TO GO?

NO, BUT YOU SHOULD.

GO ON, HAVE FUN. I'LL FIND YOU THAT COTTON CANDY.
I DON'T KNOW IF THAT'S—
I'LL BE FINE. GO.
RCARS

MOTHERS AGAINST ROCK & ROLL MUSIC
WHAT WOULD YOU SAY IF I WERE TO TELL YOU . . . THAT SATAN NO LONGER FEARS THE RIGHTEOUS?
MOTHERS AGAINST ROCK & ROLL MUSIC
WHAT WOULD YOU SAY IF I WERE TO TELL YOU . . . THAT SATAN IS PREACHING HIS MESSAGE THROUGH YOUR CHILDREN'S STEREO?
WELL, BROTHERS, SISTERS, I'M SORRY, BUT THESE ARE THE FACTS.
CAN I TELL YOU HOW I KNOW THIS TO BE TRUE?

MY OWN DAUGHTER, A GIRL WHO NEVER STRAYED FROM THE PATH A DAY IN HER LIFE, IS AFFLICTED BY THE DEVIL'S MUSIC.

SHE AND HER FRIENDS ORGANIZED PARTIES IN THE WOODS, WHERE THEY WOULD LISTEN TO ROCK-AND-ROLL MUSIC.

KNOWING FULL WELL THEY WERE FORBIDDEN THIS DEVIL'S MUSIC IN THEIR GOD-FEARING HOMES.

WELL, TONIGHT I BROUGHT THOSE RECORDS I FOUND IN MY DAUGHTER'S POSSESSION.

TONIGHT I'M GOING TO PLAY THEM FOR YOU SO THAT YOU UNDERSTAN HOW SATAN IS TRYING T SEDUCE YOUR CHILDREN

BUT BE WARNED, YOU WILL NEED THE LOVE OF GOD IN YOUR HEART IF YOU ARE TO HEAR THE DEVIL'S SONG FOR WHAT IT IS.

TONIGHT I WILL BURN THE RECORDS I HAVE FOUND IN MY OWN HOME, HIDING IN THE DARKNESS, UNDER MY DAUGHTER'S BED.

BUT FIRST LET ME PLAY YOU A PORTION. SO THAT YOU MAY HEAR THE LURE OF SATAN FOR YOURSELVES, AND STEEL YOURSELVES AGAINST IT.

MOMMA, NO!

DON'T YOU SEE, MILLIE? I MUST.

TO PROTECT YOU.

BURN THEM IF YOU WANT! SMASH THEM TO A MILLION BITS, I DON'T CARE.
JUST DON'T PLAY THAT ONE.
LET THAT SONG BE THE FIRST INTO THE FIRE.
I'M SO PROUD OF YOU, DAUGHTER, FOR REPENTING AS YOU HAVE.
BUT I HAVE TO.
WE MUST KNOW WHAT IT IS WE ARE FIGHTING AGAINST.

Cotton

NO, NO, NO.
I FEEL IT. THE SONG.
WHERE'S AL? WHERE DID AL GO?
HE WAS GOING TO GET COTTON CANDY.

AL!
AAAAAAL!
AL . . .
MOTHERS AGAINST ROCK & ROLL MUSIC

Mothers Against Rock & Roll Music

SSKRRRK
SMASH!

ALWAYS MOVED FROM TASK TO TASK,
BEEN AFRAID OF WANTING MORE.
NEVER STOPPED SO LONG TO ASK . . .
WHAT IT IS I'M LOOKING FOR.

DO YOU THINK THAT YOU MIGHT STAY?
OR BE GONE LONG BEFORE?
YOU'RE GONNA GIVE ME THE CHANCE TO SAY . . .
YOU'RE THE ONE THAT I ADORE.
WHEN I SAW YOU, YOUR MELODY . . .
WHEN I SAW YOU, SWEET HARMONY . . .

I CAN'T STOP YOU . . .
FROM DESTROYING ME . . .
BUT WOULD I IF I COULD?
OH, WOULD I IF I COULD?

HOLY SHIT, IT WORKED.
IT ACTUALLY WORKED!
YOU DID IT! YOU STOPPED IT!
HOW DID YOU DO THAT?

AL? ARE YOU OKAY?
WAS I JUST SAVED BY A LOVE SONG?
EW.
TUNNEL of LOVE
WHERE WERE YOU?

AND WHAT THE HELL ARE YOU DOING HERE NOW?
I WENT TO DESTROY ONE OF THE RECORDS IN BOSTON. THE ONE THAT HURT AL.
I'M NOT SURE WHAT YOU KNOW ABOUT ME, PETE. BUT PEOPLE HAVE DIED BECAUSE OF ME.
I KNOW.

AND YOU DON'T HATE ME?
I'M DEVASTATED. FOR THOSE PEOPLE. FOR THEIR FAMILIES.
BUT DID YOU KNOW WHAT YOU WERE DOING WHEN YOU RECORDED THAT SONG?
I SWEAR I DIDN'T. I STILL DON'T UNDERSTAND IT.
I WANT TO HELP YOU UNDERSTAND IT.
MY FAMILY CAN HELP YOU.

BUT THE SONG. WHY THAT SONG? HOW DID YOU KNOW IT WOULD WORK?
I DIDN'T. I JUST THOUGHT . . .
I THOUGHT THAT IF MY SONG, WHICH REPRESENTED SO MUCH DREAD AND LOSS, WAS HARMING PEOPLE . . .
MAYBE YOUR SONG WHICH MADE ME FEE BETTER THAN I HAV IN A VERY, VERY LON TIME, MIGHT HELP HEAL THEM.
YOU HELPED ME, PETE. WHEN I THOUGHT I WAS BEYOND IT.
SO YOU'RE A WITCH?
NOT EXACTLY. I MEAN, SOMETHING LIKE THAT.
I'M LEARNING.
CAN YOU LAY A MAGICAL ASS-KICKING LIKE RACHEL?
YOU GOT SECRETS, PETER MONTAGUE.
YES. WELL. SORT OF.

I THINK YOU MIGHT OWE ME SOME ROYALTIES.

CHAPTER 6

ELL, THAT'S BOSS. CAN WE GET ONE OF THESE DOORS FOR THE HOUSE?
I KNOW IT SEEMS LIKE A GOOD IDEA, BUT JUST WAIT TILL THE FIRST TIME YOU HAVE A BIT TOO MUCH SHERRY, COME HOME, AND CAN'T REMEMBER YOUR PASSWORD. HIGHLY IMPRACTICAL.
WHEN DID THIS PLACE BURN DOWN, AGAIN?

CORRECT ME IF I'M WRONG, DAVID, BUT I BELIEVE IT WAS '54.
THAT'S CORRECT.
A STUDENT PROTEST GOT OUT OF HAND.
ASK YOUR MOTHER ABOUT IT SOMETIME.
REMEMBER TO ONLY SPEAK THE TRUTH. THE SHADOWS WILL CALL OUT A LIE.
AND DON'T TRY TO SPEAK FOR SOMEONE ELSE. THEY HATE THAT.
WATCH YOURSELVES. THIS PART CAN BE A LITTLE TRICKY.

AHHHSSSSONNNOFABITCH, THAT STINGS. OOH, THAT'S AD. IT'S BARELY BLEEDING. OW DOES IT HURT SO BAD?

I THOUGHT MY HAND WOULD GO RIGHT THROUGH THEM!

I SAID TO WATCH YOURSELF, NOT STICK YOUR HAND INTO THE WHIRLING CYCLONE OF PAPER.

WHY?!

WE'LL BE RIGHT OUT HERE.

WHAT IF WE SOMEHOW GET YOU GUYS, AND OURSELVES, INTO TROUBLE?

PETE, DON'T YOU WORRY ABOUT THAT.

YOU'VE ALREADY CAUSED THE TROUBLE.

AND I'M SO PROUD OF YOU ALL.
DITTO.
NOW GET IN THERE. YOU'LL DO GREAT.
WE'RE GETTING BANISHED, AREN'T WE?
THERE'S A STRONG LIKELIHOOD, YES.
COOL, COOL, COOL.

APPROACH.
DO YOU KNOW WHY YOU HAVE BEEN CALLED?
YES.
YOU CHILDREN ARE INVOLVED IN SOMETHING VERY DANGEROUS.
HAVE THE HAZARDS OF PRACTICING MAGIC BEEN IMPARTED TO YOU?
YES.
IT SEEMS ALL OF YOU HAVE A CONNECTION TO OUR BOARD IN SOME WAY.
DO YOU UNDERSTAND YOUR OWN HISTORIES?
YES.

YE YES YES YES YES YES
NO.
BUT THEN, HOW COULD YOU?
WE HAVE DECIDED THAT WE WILL PERMIT YOU TO CONTINUE YOUR STUDIES.
HOWEVER, THEY WILL NO LONGER BE THE UNSANCTIONED FREE-FOR-ALL YOU HAVE BECOME ACCUSTOMED TO.
THEY WILL BE RIGOROUS. DOUBLE THE WORK OF YOUR CURRENT ACADEMIC SCHEDULE. YOU MUST PERFORM TO EXCEPTIONAL LEVELS, BOTH THERE AND HERE.
IN A SHORT TIME, EACH OF YOU WILL BE OF AGE TO ENROLL AT THE UNIVERSITY.
YOU WI DO SC

CAN ROWAN STILL TEACH US? WHAT ABOUT DAVID?
THEY WILL.
WHAT'S THAT?
THERE HAS BEEN A REQUEST. A MEMBER OF THE FACULTY ON THE SIDE OF THE INQUISITORS WISHES TO SPEAK TO PETER AND ALASTAIR IN PRIVATE.
THIS SESSION WILL BE ADJOURNED TO PERMIT THEIR REQUEST.
THE FACULTY WILL BE IN TOUCH.

YOU'RE WELCOME.
THERE WERE SOME PRETTY HORRIFIC PUNISHMENTS ON THE TABLE FOR ALL OF YOU. ESPECIALLY FOR ROWAN AND DAVID.
I INTERVENED ON YOUR BEHALF.
AND WHY WOULD YOU DO THAT?

I AM NOT THE NSTER YOU MAY E HEARD ABOUT.
I HAVE A LOT TO EXPLAIN TO YOU BOTH. ALL I ASK IS THAT I'M GIVEN THAT OPPORTUNITY.
NOT HERE. I DON'T WANT TO FORCE YOU INTO A CONVERSATION YOU DON'T WANT TO HAVE.
I JUST HAVE ONE QUESTION FOR YOU BOTH.
DO YOU REALLY WANT TO DO THIS? DO YOU REALLY WANT TO LEARN MAGIC?
YES.
ES YE ES YES YES

INTERESTING.

Mental Health Resources

RESOURCES IN THE U.S.

The Jed Foundation is a national nonprofit that exists to protect the emotional health of—and to prevent suicide among—our nation's teens and young adults. You can find more information at jedfoundation.org.

The National Suicide Prevention Lifeline provides 24/7 free and confidential support for people in distress, prevention and crisis resources for you or your loved ones, and best practices for professionals. You can find out more at suicidepreventionlifeline.org. If you need help now, text "START" to 741-741 to immediately connect with help at the Jed Foundation or call 1-800-273-TALK (8255) for free, confidential services with the Jed Foundation and the National Suicide Prevention Lifeline.

The Trevor Project is the leading national organization providing crisis intervention and suicide prevention services to lesbian, gay, bisexual, transgender, queer, and questioning young people under age twenty-five. The Trevor Project has a staff of trained counselors available for support 24/7. If you are in crisis, feeling suicidal, or in need of a safe and judgment-free place to talk, call the TrevorLifeline now at 1-800-488-7386 or text "START" to 678-678.

RESOURCES IN CANADA

To contact the Canada Suicide Prevention Service, call 1-833-456-4566 or text 45645 from 4 p.m. to midnight EST daily.

Crisis Services Canada (CSC) is a national network of existing distress, crisis, and suicide prevention line services. They are committed to supporting any person living in Canada who is affected by suicide, in the most caring and least intrusive manner possible. For more information, visit crisisservicescanada.ca.

To contact the Youthspace Text Line (across Canada), text 778-783-0177 from 6 p.m. to midnight PST daily.

Anyone in Canada under thirty years old is welcome to chat with a diverse community of trained volunteers.

They encourage and welcome all youth to contact them, no matter their background, religion, race, ability, sexual orientation, gender identity, lifestyle, or culture. Youthspace's goal is to create inclusive and safer spaces for all visitors to Youthspace.ca.

Acknowledgments

Every project has its heroes behind the scenes, and during such a wild year, we needed all the help we could get. Here's to our amazing team for your dedication and hard work. As always, we would be nowhere without our amazing agent, Maria Vicente, who possesses a magic far beyond that of even David. To our editor, Marisa: thank you for guiding us through the tangled garden of this story and for all your invaluable insights. Thanks so much to Joan Lee and Heather Mullan for your color-flatting mastery. To Maggie Stiefvater and Sam Maggs for saying such nice things; your encouragement means more than you could ever know. Thanks to the entire team at Knopf and Random House Graphic for the tireless job they do, not just for our books but for the medium at large. And, of course, to our support network of friends and family, without whom the Montague Twins could not exist. Thank you. We love you all.